To Free The Dragon's Soul

Book 3 – Dragons, Griffons and Centaurs, Oh My!

By: Margaret Taylor

To Quri -
Enjoy!!

Margaret
Taylor

Margaret Taylor

Dedication

For my Mother, who always believed in my talent and never let me quit.
May you rest in peace, Margaret P., December, 2003.

I would like to acknowledge and deeply thank my cousin Jana for all her loving support and belief in my work. Without her I'd have given up long ago...

To my Cover Designer, Carey, I love you...you get me! Thanks for that.

And to Ms. Grace, for always being patient with me! You are the best!

And thanks to Dr. Monica for helping with the blurb! Love you darlin'!

And to my very lovely Beta's: Robin, Frances, Patti, Karen, Anna, Kerri and Jana! Thank you ladies, you ROCK and make me want to keep writing! Love you!

Chapter One

"Well *someone* has to go!"

"It will not be you."

"Why not? I'm the only one who can, Draven. We both know it."

Fyris Taraxus stood on the sidelines watching the pair argue. He tried not to smile, really, but he'd never heard his nest mate being stood up to before.

It was a refreshing change.

The former King of Bra'ka snorted and crossed his arms. He leaned back against the balcony and tilted a regal look down his nose. "You will *not* go, *Kyleri*. I cannot allow it."

Terra Heegan planted her feet and crossed her own arms, returning Draven's look with a pinched glare. "You cannot?" she growled.

For once in his long life, the recently dethroned monarch looked a bit scared at the tone from his lover and the next potential Queen. But, he recovered in that graceful way only a sovereign who'd dealt with hundreds of diplomats and regents would. "I cannot," he said again. He pushed off the railing, nostrils flaring. "As Ruler, it is my duty to keep you safe. It is too dangerous."

Draven pulled the 'King card' and he bit back on a hard laugh, covering it with an equally hard cough. Molten orange eyes, almost the exact color as his own, swung his way and he waved a hand in front of his nose. "Sorry. Must be something in the air."

His kin snorted, turned back to his lady and one eyebrow quirked in the air.

He shifted around enough to fully see her face and

couldn't help but wince himself.

She was furious. Flames snapped to life around her clenched fist and began creeping up her arm. Her silver eyes danced with blue specks and she drew in a long breath, a muscle along the bottom of her jaw ticking wildly. "Fine," she said through clenched teeth. "What would *you* suggest, Your *Highness*?"

Oh boy...Draven had royally stepped in this one. Only the poor man didn't seem to know it.

His shoulders pulled back. "We will find someone else."

The flames edged up to her elbow, dancing and twisting along her skin. "Who..."

Draven turned desperate eyes his way and he shook his head, smiling smugly. He wasn't about to travel to the human world, king or not.

"Fyris can do it. Or Arin, or, or, or..."

Terra twisted a look over her shoulder and he again, shook his head, dropping the smug smile. He'd seen what her fire could do during the battle to take back Bra'ka and he just wasn't up to tempting fate, this daylight at least. He'd done that enough in his 400+ Suns and didn't relish the idea of being roasted alive.

She turned back when he said nothing. "It would be sending a lamb to slaughter, Draven. I have to go and we both know it."

His nest mate dropped the pretense, finally, and closed the distance between them. "*Kyleri*, please," he said, trying reason at long last. "I know you are still angry with me for lying to you and I do not know how many times I can say I am sorry..."

The flames slithered higher, stopping just shy of her armpit and her knuckles cracked loudly. "Don't you dare try to placate me," she hissed. "I won't have it. We will discuss *that* later. I am going after Golix and that's the end of it. I owe that bastard! He killed my sister, dammit!"

With that said, she spun and stomped into the suite of rooms they'd been given when they arrived in the Harpy Capital of Win-ra.

Draven whipped the other way, gripping the railing he'd just been leaning against until it bent with an ominous rending creak.

He pushed off the door jamb, trying not to laugh outright. "She will forgive you, some daylight."

The railing suffered another twist and crunch. "I know. I just wish she would do it. This is killing me."

He patted the poor guy on the shoulder. "In her defense, you did lie about something rather large my friend."

Draven snorted softly and let go of the ruined metal with one hand to pinch the bridge of his nose. "Yes, I did. For the good of everyone, can she not see that?"

"She does, I am sure," a second male's voice commented.

He turned to find Arin Manus coming through the doorway. The Neither-Born Chimera looked much healthier than he had a couple of rotations ago. The tan had returned to his skin, his cheeks had fattened out and most of the wounds they all bore from the battle in Gommel had almost healed.

His lady was right behind him. Haydn Durel's blue-red eyes went to Draven and she shook her head slowly. Easing under Arin's arm, the former Orc Assassin sighed hard. "She is still upset I take it?"

Draven nodded. "So much so, she wants to return home, find Golix and kill him."

The Orc's head tilted slightly. "And what is wrong with that? She deserves the honor."

Fyris answered before anyone else. "You all deserve the honor. That black son of a War Dog put you through the Nether Worlds and back again. However, Draven fears if she leaves, she will not return."

The Orc and Chimera both grunted but it was Arin that spoke. Dropping a hand on his friends back, he gave it a hard squeeze. "She loves you. You are Mates. She would return."

Draven's head lifted and he stared out over the city. "Of that I am not so sure, old friend. She hates me."

There was a hitch there and he sighed, bailing his nest mate out of the situation before it got worse. For anyone. "Oh fine. I will go."

The King's head whipped around, long black hair flying out and there was relief in the molten orange of his eyes. "You would do that for me?"

He finally did laugh. Throwing back his head, he let go of the amusement he'd been keeping in check since they'd started bantering back and forth at the crack of daylight. "Oh good Gods no. You still owe me for saving your scaly hide in Syrax all those Suns ago." He jerked a nod in the direction Terra had gone. "I will go for her."

Draven's brows pinched together. "Why?"

He shrugged. "I like her."

"You do?" Arin asked.

The Chimera's golden eyes were full of shock and rightfully so. He didn't *like* anyone usually.

"I do." Still smiling, he jerked a thumb at Draven.

"She stands up to him."

***

"So, where are we?"

Arin sighed at Draven's question and for just a brief thump of his twin hearts, debated about lying. But he'd never done it before, no reason to start now. "It is not good. Haydn has spent the last rotations in touch with her contacts and there is nothing. No word on Lanni, no sightings, no, well, just nothing."

Draven came out on to the balcony and pillowed his forearms on the railing. "Did they find the ship?"

He joined his best friend, propping his chin on a fist. "Yes. But there was no sign of survivors. Not even the crew. It was empty."

Draven's head swung around. "That could be good, yes?"

There was such hope in his eyes, that he wanted to lie, he really did, but giving false hope had never been his forte, so he didn't. "Or bad. We do not even know she was on the ship. We only have a third hand account of what happened on that roof, Draven. We have no way to confirm any of it."

The brief flicker of optimism melted away and he hated himself for just a moment. "Look, I am not saying it is not possible she survived. But from Tane's account of events, even if she did, she has most likely passed now."

Draven's hands wrapped around the metal and the recently repaired Rustac suffered his wrath a second time. "And that does not bother you?"

He clenched his hands into fists. "Of course it

bothers me you son of a *Nawi*! I loved her! If anyone wants to go running back to Bra'ka and tear the place apart, it is me! Do not ever doubt that…"

The King hung his head, his chest expanding slowly. "I know, I am sorry." He twisted a pained look back over his shoulder toward the dark interior of their suite. "It is just that, I hoped, I wanted," he stammered.

Arin let go of his anger on a long burst of air and patted him on the shoulder, commiserating with the poor guy over the state of his love life. Terra hadn't said more than six words to him in the last rotations and even those were snipped and cold.

And he couldn't blame the woman. She had a right to her anger. The man she trusted above all, had lied outright and kept her sisters state to himself. Not only that, he hadn't even had a chance to tell her the truth. It had come from Furiem Corlant, the Royal Reporter that had escaped the city to warn them Lanni was connected to the attacking ships through magic and with each they destroyed, they were killing her.

It wasn't until they retreated, that Haydn had seen the message from Cannis seeking the human woman. She investigated further, the Gods love her and found a brief message from one of the Royal Guards, Tane, stating Phara Sylor, Lanni and some Half-Ogre, Half-Harpy thing had managed to escape on one of Golix's ships.

He had no idea why Cannis still wanted her though but it was a matter for later.

He patted Draven on the back again, giving his best friend what he could. "Look, Tian Dyran and his team are on the way. If anyone can get into the city and find out more, they can. It is the best we can do, for now.

Once we know what we are truly dealing with, we will come up with a plan."

***

"Talk to me *Kyleri*, please?"

Terra couldn't bring herself to look at him and continued to stare out over the lit trees and buildings below their balcony. She had to admit, at any other time, she would have enjoyed the view.

Win-ra, the Harpy capital, was beautiful and the first real indication she'd seen since arriving in the Five Kingdoms that this was a completely different world than her own. Prior to now everything she'd been exposed too, was as modern as anything she'd grown up with. But this city, wasn't. Situated in the center of a massive jungle, equally massive trees had been turned into buildings. Catwalks of Rustac stretched from one to another and most had been hollowed out to form offices, shops, and residential living space.

The sun had set hours ago, but even so, the bird-like creatures walked along the thoroughfares, going here and there on whatever business they had. She'd only seen a few non-Harpies so far, her party included, and Arin had told her they didn't usually allow strangers to live among them, for long anyway.

The Harpies preferred to keep to themselves and she could understand that. Right now, she felt much the same. She desperately wanted a quiet place to think, to decide when she could forgive the man she loved or even *if* she could.

But she didn't have a private place. Instead, they'd stuffed her, Draven, Arin and Haydn into a suite that

9

was only slightly bigger than her apartment back home. They had separate bedrooms, fortunately, a living room, a kitchen of sorts, though she had yet to figure out how to operate the appliances, a bathroom and what equated to a small office.

Not a lot of space to fume and be pissy, but she'd managed by staying in the office mostly. From sunrise to sunset, she'd been glued to what they called the Blacknet, looking for anything about Lanni or what might be happening in Bra'ka. Sadly there wasn't much. An occasional posting to the message boards from the citizens trapped under the dome, or a brief news bulletin from the bastard running the show, Tyleios Cannis. Beyond that, nothing.

Drawing in a lungful of dry air, she finally answered his soft entreaty. "What do you want me to say, Draven?"

There was an audible gulp. "That you will forgive me?"

Oh, the question of the day. Could she? Did she even want too? She had no idea. "You lied to me."

She crossed her arms, more in defense of her heart than anything else and finally turned. The molten orange eyes that usually set her on fire were sad, desperate and maybe even a little angry, though whether it was directed at her or himself, she couldn't be sure. But, it was enough for her to finally voice all the stuff she'd pent up for the last 12 days.

"You lied to me," she said again. "And not in the 'Hey babe, I pick my nose and eat it' sort of way." Anger raged along her nerves and she closed the small space between them, poking him in the chest with a stiff finger. "Or the, 'Hey babe, I leave the seat up' or 'Hey, honey, I ate a Goblin today, you ok with that?'"

He took a step back, his jaw tightening on a crack.

She poked him again. Now that she'd gotten started, she wasn't going to stop until she got it all out. "No, you *lied* about my *sister*, you half-breed son of a Unicorn!" Ok, that wasn't true, but it was the best derisive curse she could come up with in the heat of the moment. "You let me go on believing for days, *days* that she was dead when you knew damn good and well she might not be!"

He took another step back, his nostrils flaring. "In my defense," he whispered through clenched teeth. "We had bigger problems at the time."

"Bigger problems? Tell me what is bigger than family?!"

He drew back his shoulders, eyes pulsing a bright red. "I was worried you would run off and try to rescue her. There, I said it. Happy?"

Her mouth flopped open.

Did he think so little of her? That she'd drop everything and head off in the face of an epic fight for their very survival to save her sister? That shook everything she thought she knew about him right down to the core.

She snapped her mouth closed, hot tears pooling in her eyes. "I see. So, just because I've bailed Lanni out of every mess in her life, you arbitrarily decided, I'd do the same thing this time?"

He gulped again, eyes widening at her choice of phrasing. "Well, yes, I did."

She swiped angrily at the water coursing down her cheeks, refusing to let her bottom lip quiver. "If you had told me, or even asked me, I would have said it was one

11

mess I couldn't personally do a damn thing about. Not right then anyway." She stole a breath out of the air and added, "I would have found another way though. Maybe asked Mithrin to return and see what he could do, or if he knew someone else to send."

He blinked, his eyes fluctuating through a myriad of colors so quickly she couldn't even begin to name them all.

"But, the plain fact of the matter is, you didn't trust me enough to do that. You didn't trust our relationship, or my love for you, that I might make the right choice and stand by your side." She poked him one final time as she walked past. "*That* is what I don't know if I can forgive or not..."

Chapter Two

Rygan Turosh paced along the catwalk, his wings fluttering.

"That is not helping."

He spun, glaring at the Naiad casually leaning against the wall. "Maybe not, but it does make me feel, useful."

A blonde eyebrow rose. "By wearing a hole in the plating?"

He crossed his arms. "It would give…" He started but was interrupted by the door next to them opening.

Rinsa, one of the few Harpy's to survive the onslaught, stepped out, his eyes tired. He scrubbed a feather covered hand down his beak and let out a weary sigh. "I have done what is possible."

Phara pushed off the wall. "And?"

The doctor turned a sad look over his shoulder toward the room he'd just exited. "And, what?" His gaze came back around to the two of them. "Without the proper equipment, all I can really do is make her comfortable."

He shifted a step to see the figure in the bed for himself. What machines they'd managed to pilfer from the local residents inhabiting the network caves and caverns under Bra'ka beeped softly, monitoring what few vitals remained. Heart rate, blood pressure, all the usual things one needed to live. There was only one problem, the pale human wasn't living, at least not much. She was existing, breathing, but beyond that she hadn't moved since they'd arrived.

"What do you need?" Phara asked.

He turned back to the conversation.

Rinsa scratched at the dirty feathers on his neck. "Well, for starters, human blood. A lot of it. She lost the majority of hers and what little is left, is fighting some infection I have never seen before." He dropped his hands into the pockets of his once white lab coat. "I could probably counter it, if she was in the Shi-so...or," he paused and huffed out another long sigh. "If I had some medicines from back home." He swung a look off to the left, toward the underground complex they'd managed to get too after the ship crashed. "Down here does not have much to offer."

Rygan couldn't disagree with that. The Halfling Undermarket wasn't the place to find the latest of anything, much less life-saving medicines or technologies. But, it was safe, for now, from the horde of Ogre's, Orcs, Griffons and Centaurs currently inhabiting Bra'ka.

Ok, they weren't exactly inhabiting, not peacefully anyway. No, they'd taken the place, spilling through the gates in a swath of destruction and darkness no one was ready for.

Commanded by the Interim King, Tyleios Cannis, they'd spent the last 12 rotations raping and pillaging their way through the 300,000 some odd citizens that had co-existed behind the walls for eons. Those same citizens had tried to defend themselves, but they weren't fighters and had quickly cow-towed to the massive and sadly, superior force. Martial Law was immediately instituted and anyone caught on the streets after darkfall was summarily executed, or from the rumors rampaging through the Undermarket, worse.

"I could go get help."

This came from a small ferret perched atop the Naiad's shoulder and he glared at it. "You know a way out of the city?"

The ferret rose on his hind legs and nodded quickly. "Yes. It is not easy, but doable. Furiem showed me."

Phara Sylor turned toward him. "Will it get us past the shield and the guards?"

She was referring to the dome Golix, the evil bastard of a Unicorn, had created over Bra'ka itself with spell magic. It was impenetrable, unless you were coated with a certain human's blood and she didn't have a whole lot of it left.

It was the spell that had nearly killed her and while they'd managed to pull her from its dark clutches, a great cost had been paid. A very good friend of his had sacrificed himself when he'd taken her place...

He coughed back a fresh round of tears and squared his shoulders. "I will go. Show me."

Phara's eyes came around to his, narrowing into small slits. She was still pissed over Garax's death and he couldn't blame her. It was all his fault. If he hadn't been so vain as to allow Golix to control him, none of this would have happened. "You have done enough. You stay here and out of the way."

He wanted to argue, but she was right. All he ever did was make things worse. Always had. "Fine." He swung around to the doctor. "What can I do?"

The Harpy dug a data stone out of his pocket and handed it to Phara. "Give this to the Crone Mother. She will know what to send back with you. As for you," he snarled. "As she said, stay out of the way."

With that he headed back into the room they'd converted into a sick bed of sorts for Lanni Heegan...

***

Phara eyed the small drainage pipe then gave the Ferret on her shoulder a skeptical look. "Are you sure about this?"

Her companion nodded, his brown whiskers twitching. "It ends near Chenna Lake."

She stole a nervous breath, which filled her mouth with nasty sewage and coughed it back out again. "I swear, if you are wrong, I will pluck the fur from your body."

The mammal laughed and patted her cheek. "I promise, you will come out beyond the shield and the guards will not see you."

With another skeptical look and a sniff, she set him aside, got down on all fours and crawled into the pipe barely large enough to fit through. The grossest water ever slimed over and between her fingers and quickly coated her from the thighs down.

If she lived through this, she was going to kill that half-ogre, half-harpy! She was going to pluck the feathers from his wings, one by one and make a hat! She was going to flay him alive and use his skin for a new door! She was going to...

Well, she didn't know what else, but the thoughts were enough to get her through the half-a-length's worth of grunge and muck.

Rolling out on the other side, she stood and drew in a deep lungful of clean air. For half a heartbeat she debated going for a swim to wash off the filth but never got the chance.

"You there! Stop!"

Whipping around, she spied six brutish Ogre's pounding down the hill from above and had only one choice.

Run.

She bolted for the pristine lake, ignoring the first arrow that bounced off her armor. The second was not so easy to forget. Piercing through her arm, she growled and wanted to turn and fight.

But, she didn't dare take the time. Another life was at stake and brawling with six of the beasts was a senseless waste. It was better to get away, live to fight another rotation and all that.

Her boots pounded across the grass, her heart drummed in her chest, her breath frosted against the air and feet from the water's edge, she launched toward the glass-like calmness, hoping it was deep enough to dive under and disappear.

Pain radiated through her calf and thigh and she hissed, barely able to draw in enough air before she splashed through the surface. She stroked, pulling at the water with her working arm and sunk toward the bottom, letting her lungs fill as she went.

She would love to have Zesul around right about now, but had no idea where her mount might have ended up. She hadn't seen him since they'd snuck on board Golix's flying ships near the West Beach, so he was most likely back home.

Neither here nor there really, she'd just have to swim for it and hope she made it before she passed out...

***

There had to be something he could do. This was all his fault after all, so surely he could do…more than just stand around looking out of place and forlorn over the events.

Right?

Right!

Reaching up, he scratched Tollo under the chin. "What do you think? Should I head topside and see if I can find something to help?"

The Ilthe stirred from where he'd been sleeping in the crook of his neck, stretched and blinked his little bug eyes. One of them widened a bit and he repeated the question.

"*Purr, purr, trill, growl, purr, trill, trill…*" Tollo replied around a wide, teeth filled yawn.

Rygan sighed. "You know I do not understand you, you blasted little beast."

"He said, yes, you should get off your winged rear and fix this."

He turned toward the new voice and crooked a smile. "You know, your father understood him too. So, fine, what do the two of you suggest I do?"

Niar Corlant bounded across the railings of the catwalk, scurried up his leg and perched on his other shoulder. Tapping his chin, his ferret features frowned deeply, looking exactly like his father, Furiem. "Let us see, the good Doctor said he might be able to help your human friend if he had medicine from the Shi-So Medical Center, yes?"

He tilted a look toward the room, watching the doctor checking Lanni's vitals by hand. "That he did. But he did not say what he needed. At least to me."

One of Niar's small hands smacked against his right cheek and Tollo's slobbery tongue smacked him on the left.

"Ok, ok, fine, I will ask."

He wiped the goop off and pushed off the railing. Leaning in the doorway, he tried not to look at the figure in the bed. Doing so would only break his heart all over again. He cleared his throat to gain the Harpies attention. "Doctor? You said there were things in the Med Center that would help. Could you make me a list?"

The blue-green feather-covered head swung his way and his eyes pinched into a glare. "I will not. Do you not think you have caused enough trouble, Half-Breed?"

He couldn't deny that but stood his ground. For once. "That is true, which is why it falls to me to do what I can to help. Now, make a list, if you please."

The Harpy snorted but reached for the board hanging from the end of the bed. Flipping through the sheets it contained, he found a blank one and began writing. He scribbled for a long while, the scratching of the pen adding a weird cadence to the softly beeping machines in the background. Eventually he ripped the paper free and held it out.

He took it and his eyes widened as they scanned over the contents. "You need all this?"

The doctor tucked his hands in his pockets, his shoulders slumping slightly. "That is the ideal list, yes. But, in reality, if you can procure the top five, that would at least give her a fighting chance."

He folded the paper and tucked it into the pouch on his belt. "I will do my best in that case." Scooping

Tollo off his shoulder, he held him up to eye level. "Will you keep an eye on our friend?"

"*Trill, purr, trill.*"

Niar hopped down his arm and joined the Ilthe on his palm. "We both will. Now, go, before it gets dark up there. If they catch you out and about, you are likely to end up feeding the shield from what I hear…"

***

The voices drifted across the darkness of Lanni's mind and she tried to focus on them. But they were muffled, distant, like a vid playing in another room. No matter how much she strained to make out what they were saying, they were just too far away.

Not to mention the effort hurt like hell.

Shit, everything hurt. Her body was on fire, but it wasn't a flash heat. No, it was a slow, deliberate, smoldering burn that was eating her alive. From the inside.

As silly as it sounded, she tried to talk to the blaze. *I'm so very tired. Go away!*

She didn't expect a reply, but a strong, firm voice countered her plea.

I cannot. You need me.

No, I don't. Leave me be!

Yes, you do. Without me, you will die.

Internally, she sighed. *What if I want to die?* She asked.

You cannot. It is not your time.

She frowned at that. Or at least she wanted too but her face muscles didn't move that she could tell. *It's too much. It burns. Make it stop.*

20

The voice chuckled. *The burn is keeping you alive, Chilani.*

Who are you?

It didn't answer and she thought she was alone again. Which sucked. She didn't want to be alone, not anymore. She wanted Mithrin, or Terra, or Arin, or hell even Draven would have been preferable to this, this darkness. Anyone to hold her and tell her it was going to be alright.

It will be alright.

A soft purring roved across the blackness and she realized who she'd been talking too finally.

The little furball that had kept her company on the ship. It had to be.

What's your name?

I am Tollo.

How, how is this possible? Are you, telepathic or something?

The voice chuckled again. *Not in the way you are thinking. But, I did roll in your blood, so a connection was established.*

Something warm and furry snuggled down against her neck and the purring increased, soothing her. *Where are we?* She finally thought to ask.

Safe. For now. Just hold on. Help is on the way. It will get better.

Are you sure?

As I can be.

She laughed, maybe, well, she wanted too, but even that hurt. At least the little guy was being honest. Another question popped into her head. *What are you?*

I am Ilthe.

And that is?

21

Another chuckle and she felt his tongue gently lick at her cheek. *We are Guardians.*

Of?

Whomever is in need at the time, but mostly, we look after the Dragons...

Chapter Three

"What is that?"

Tian swiveled the direction Dain, his second in command was pointing. In the distance, a glint of metal caught the first rays of daylight peeking through the trees. "I am unsure. I shall look. Stay here."

He had no doubt his orders would be followed and shifted into his humanoid version. Ducking through the foliage, he made no sound as he worked his way to the water's edge. His team of Chimera had been moving along the river that fed out of Chenna Lake for the last six rotations, hoping it would lead them to a way into Bra'ka. It would be another two before they reached the city proper and this was a distraction he didn't need, but metal this far out deserved a cursory glance, if nothing else.

It was probably some left over wreckage from the battle, but still...

Stopping at the edge of the trees, he blinked several times, wondering if the body in front of him was dead or alive. It certainly looked dead, it wasn't moving and had three arrows sticking out of it.

It was just another casualty. Turning away, a moan drew him back and he was surprised to see it heave itself over onto its side. Unbelievably it pushed up onto its hands and knees and started to crawl away from the water's edge toward the trees in which he hid.

It, no, wait, she made it about halfway across the stretch of dirt then collapsed with a pained grunt. She panted, coughed up some water and tried again. On shaky arms and legs, she made a few more inches and was done.

He waited several thumping heartbeats and thought she might have died but she moaned and managed to heave herself over again. Pushing her soaked hair off her face, she coughed violently and gave one more valiant effort to get to the tree line.

Dragging herself along with one arm, she almost made it before whatever she'd been through took its toll. She closed her eyes and passed out with a soft whimper he almost missed.

Something tugged at his twin hearts. He shouldn't interfere though. He didn't have the time, but there was something in the effort she'd put into getting up the bank that impressed him.

Breaking cover, he carefully made his way across the dirt and gently scooped her up into his arms. Her blood trickled down his front and he knew at least one of the shafts had hit something major. She'd most likely bleed out before he even got back to the others.

"What is that?" Dain asked when he did arrive.

He chuckled. "A female."

His second snorted, the left head shaking. "I can see," it said. "That," the right added. "What is it doing," the left said. "Here?" the right finished.

He set her down, careful of the bolts. "How should I know? She washed up on shore."

"Is she dead?" one of the others asked.

"Not yet. Who has the medkit?"

***

The soft tap, tap, tap of water on canvas drew Phara Sylor back to the land of the living. She really wished it hadn't though. She wasn't ready for the burning pain pulsing through her blood, or the deep, bone chilling cold that followed it.

She shivered violently and tried to burrow under whatever covering someone had wrapped her in.

"She needs something to counter the toxin."

"I know."

Another wave of hot-cold circulated through her body and she couldn't have stopped the moan from crossing her lips if she wanted to.

And she did. She was a Warrior, by the Gods! She didn't moan. She didn't whimper or cry or kick and scream in pain.

She dealt with it.

But this, this was worse than that time she was almost eaten by a Black. Or the time she'd tried to take on a Carnivore by herself and nearly been drowned for the trouble of it. Or that time she'd...

"We should take her to her people."

"Do you know where the Naiad's live?"

"Well, no, but we could find them."

There was a sad hitch in the responding voice. "She would never make it."

They were barely loud enough for her to hear over the pitter-pat of rain but she cracked an eye, seeking them out through the foggy haze. She licked dry lips and shakily pushed back the covering. More pain contorted its way up from her legs and she sucked hot air into her lungs. Blinking slowly, she tried to make out the area through the haze of her fever.

She was in a tent, of sorts. Actually it looked more like a wide piece of canvas had been thrown over a rope strung between two trees. One end lifted slightly and a tall, if fuzzy figure ducked under it.

"What are you doing?"

She groaned at her own weakness and steadied herself as best she could. "I, must go." She managed to push to her feet but her legs blazed with fire and buckled.

Strong arms caught her and a rumbling chuckle tickled her ear. "You are going nowhere."

"I must," she insisted, pushing weakly at his shoulder.

He scooped an arm under her legs and sat on small cot she'd just been laying on, keeping her tucked against his wide chest. "You will not."

The blanket or fur returned and she burrowed into his shoulder, trying to still the shake in her limbs. "Must, get, to, Win-ra."

He folded the covering tighter and sweat beaded along her upper lip and forehead. "And why is that?"

She swallowed at the desert in her mouth and tried again to push away. "Dying. Need medicine."

A large hand gently wiped the sweat from her face. "Yes, you are."

She sighed and really wanted to slap him, whomever he was. "Not me, you *losra*. Human. Lanni. Dying."

His entire frame stiffened and she could feel his eyes boring into hers even though she couldn't quite make them out over the heat of whatever was afflicting her.

"What did you say?"

She worked up more saliva and tried again. "Lanni. In City. Dying." She wormed a hand around under the covering, searching for the data stone Rinsa had given

26

her. A moment of panic set in when she couldn't find it then it dropped from under the edge of her breastplate. Clutching it, she snaked her hand free of the fur and held it out. "Give, Crone Mother."

***

Mithrin Sylor watched the family of blacks swim past the window just off the throne room. They looked as completely uninterested in him as he was in them and he sighed deeply.

He shouldn't be here. He should be tearing the Five Kingdoms apart, brick by brick if he had too, to find her. His heart ached, pounding against his breastbone relentlessly and he clutched a hand into his tunic. It didn't help and he sighed a second time.

"What is wrong, my son? You have been quite melancholy since your return."

Neptune's strong, confident voice drifted across the chamber ahead of the monarch's entrance but he didn't turn. He couldn't, if he did, he knew the man would see the truth in his eyes. "Nothing. I am fine, father. Did you need something?"

The ancient God stopped behind him and he caught the look of true, parental concern flitter across his features before it was shuttered away. "No. I think you are the one in need."

He steeled his own expression into a mask of indifference and finally turned. "I am fine," he said again. "Nothing to be concerned about. Now, if you do not need me, I have a patrol..."

He started to walk past the ruler he'd never questioned in a thousand Suns, but a hand shot out, resting gently on his shoulder before he could get more than a step or two.

"Son," Neptune said quietly. "Talk to me."

He drew in a long breath and tucked his hands into his armpits to keep them from forming fists. For the first time, ever, he wished his father was more understanding about the world beyond their tiny little corner of it.

He wanted to rant and rail against the ancient laws they'd lived by since before he was born.

He wanted to scream to the stalactites hanging down from above, over the injustice of it all.

He wanted to leave, right now, tell his father and the people he'd sworn to protect to go visit every level of the Nether Worlds he could think of!

But he didn't. He'd lived by and abided the same laws he was now wishing didn't exist.

"I cannot, father," he finally said.

Neptune's white-haired head tilted and he stroked the long beard with his other hand. "Why? Have you done something you should not have?"

He turned his gaze away, fixing it to a point on the far wall, carefully keeping his thoughts away from what they actually were. "No. I have not."

But, he had. He'd fallen in love, as fast and hard as the waves that crashed against the rocks of their island home. And with an outsider no less. Never mind that she was a half-human, Half-Dragon Born. She wasn't a Naiad and therefore completely off limits. No matter how much his heart and soul wished it was otherwise.

Neptune's mouth opened to reply but a pounding set of boots coming up the stairs interrupted whatever he'd been about to say.

Vor, one of the guards who regularly manned the communication room skidded to a halt at the room's entrance, a look of sheer panic in his sea-green eyes. He gulped at seeing both of them and spoke in a rush of words. "Forgive the intrusion your Majesty, your Highness. But, there is word."

The monarch turned to face the man, tilting his head in a nod for him to continue.

Vor held out a crumpled piece of parchment. "We intercepted a communication from a Chimera named Tian Dyran. He sent a message to the Crone Mother in Win-ra just moments ago." The paper shook slightly. "It is Phara."

Mithrin shifted out from under his father's hand and strode across the room, swiping the note away. He read it quickly, his heart pummeling against his ribs with each word. She was alive! According to the message, Phara needed medicine for a human who was dying in Bra'ka.

Tian had added the news about his siblings own injuries though and he latched onto that, knowing this was his only chance, ever, to fulfill the promise he'd made to Lanni on the West Beach all those rotations ago.

He turned back in Neptune's direction, lying for the second time in less than a tick to the one man he'd never even thought to deceive before now.

"My sister has been injured," he explained quietly. "This Tian requested the Harpies send along Tulzai and Teless to heal her."

Vor gulped and opened his mouth to tell their leader the rest of what the message said but he stepped in front of him to cut him off.

He waved the document to keep Neptune's attention focused his way. "They are too far away to be of help. They would not make it."

The God's forehead creased into a frown and he harrumphed softly. "Your sister does have a way of getting herself into the worst trouble."

He smiled tightly, hoping it was enough to keep his excitement hidden. "That she does. She will need Spring Water to survive. Shall I take it to her?"

Neptune's face remained furrowed and the few beats of his heart it took to make a decision were the longest of his life. "Yes. Do. And then bring her back here to recuperate."

He bowed his head and took Vor by the arm, all but dragging the poor man back out of the room. Descending the steps, he crumpled the message and tucked it into his belt. "Who else heard this?"

Vor gulped nervously, stumbling along with him. "No, no one your Highness. Just me. I brought it here as soon as I translated it."

He stopped two levels below the throne room, pulled the guard around and gripped him by the shoulders. "Tell no one what you heard. Not all of it at least. Do you understand?"

Vor's sea-green eyes darted left and right and he shook his head. "Not completely, your Highness. But, I will do as you ask."

He smiled for the first time since he'd found the prison on the beach devoid of his love. "Thank you, Vor. I owe you a bottle of Sea Grog my friend."

Vor smiled as well. "Two of them, if you please Sire."

He patted the man's shoulder and headed down

the steps again. Phara would indeed need the water from their healing spring if she was to fight off whatever toxin had coated the arrows she'd been injured with.

Within a tick of receiving the news, Mithrin was slipping through the currents, urging his oldest and dearest friend, Fancar into his fastest swim yet.

Phara knew where Lanni was and if he had any hope at all of holding to his word and rescuing her, he'd have to save his sister first...

***

Tian folded up the communication stone and tucked it back into his bag. Message sent and received. Help was on the way.

Staring down at the Naiad, he wiped the fever sweat off her brow with the sleeve of his shirt. He just hoped it was in time.

She shivered and moaned, her perfect face twisting through a myriad of emotions in her delirium. He touched her forehead, nearly jerking back from the heat wavering off her skin. Poor woman was so hot it was a wonder her skin wasn't blistering and boiling.

She bolted upright, her eyes wild and consumed with turmoil. "No, no! I will not! Stay away!"

"Shhh," he soothed, pressing her back on the makeshift cot. "You are safe."

She fought him, swinging out recklessly with both fists and shouted a string of obscenities in Naiad before reverting to a more common language again. "No! You *Nawi*! Let me be!"

The tent flap shifted and Dain's right head ducked under it. "Is all well?"

A blow caught him across the cheek before he could halt her violent outburst. He ducked a second swing and managed to gather her against his chest. "It is fine. She is dreaming."

Dain chuckled, shaking his head. "I see that. Do you need help?"

With her pinned in his arms, her feet began to flail under the fur they'd tucked around her. She growled, low and long, her heated gaze glaring death his way.

"No. We will be fine. Could use some broth though."

Dain sighed. "You will need more than broth I fear, before this is over."

He nodded slightly toward his second in command. "Most likely. But it will be a good start."

Dain harrumphed in disbelief but ducked back out of the too small tent.

Alone again, he rocked the woman, humming softly, hoping it would alleviate whatever nightmare had her in its cold, dark grip. "*Viana, tu'lin kan sil zenna...*" He sang an ancient tune his own mother had used to pacify him as kit. "*Be still my love, the dark will lift with the new daylight...You need not fear, I am here...*"

He'd forgotten the rest, but continued to hum until she stilled against his chest and her eyes slipped closed. When her breathing evened out as much as it could, he gently stretched her back out and tucked the covers around her again. For now, sweating out the toxin was the most they could do for her.

The sad part, he still didn't know her name...

Chapter Four

Fyris Taraxus was wondering what in all the Nether Worlds had possessed him to offer himself up as the sacrificial lamb in this crazy mess. Climbing slowly up the steep cliff of rocks, he wiped the sweat from his brow and shifted the pack Terra had given him.

"You know, I could lift you a bit more."

He cut a look down at Enon, resident guardian of the cave housing the portal. "No, no, I am fine. I can make it."

The massive Dragon snorted out a cloud of smoke and shook his head. He curled back to the floor, green-yellow eyes watchful. "If you say…"

"I do," he grunted.

Swinging up, he dangled by two fingers then adjusted his grip. He'd flown here from Win-ra and while both he and Enon barely fit in the cave in Dragon form, he was still too big to reach the magical opening. He'd had to shift to his humanoid self and scale it by hand. He'd tried working his way up the long bank of sand Terra and Lanni had slid down all those rotations ago, but there was no purchase to be had.

So, here he was, sweating, annoyed and about to give up on the idea when he finally reached the ledge at the top. Scrambling over, he waved, watching his fellow Dragon's scales pulse blue in relief. "I will return when I can."

Enon waved a claw. "Be safe friend. Do not let the humans bite!"

He laughed and headed deeper into the tunnel that would lead him to a world he'd grown up believing was nothing more than myth and legend.

Was he nervous?

Not really. More concerned over what the evil bastard of a Unicorn had been able to accomplish in the short time he'd been on the other side...

***

Breaking up sucked royal monkey nuts!

Fallon Togar staggered down the streets of Edinburgh, Scotland, swigging from the bottle of bourbon she'd purchased when the bartender bellowed for last call. Not normally a drinker, she was only about a third of the way into it, but it still wasn't enough to dull the pain.

In her defense, it had sounded like a good idea at the time...

Another swig, and she felt the fire-laden belch growing in her belly.

No! Not again dammit.

Swinging a look left and right she hunted for some place private. She needed a corner full of shadows that she could let loose and not worry about burning down someone's house, or yard, or business, or any number of the hundreds of things she'd set fire to in her thirty years of living with this damnable curse!

Finding nothing and fortunately no one, she leaned against the nearest streetlight, bent over and waited for it.

She'd thought she had this blasted thing under control! She hadn't had an 'incident' in almost a year now but apparently the bourbon kick started it...again.

The fire she'd lived with all her life tickled the back

of her throat. It slithered and coiled into her mouth and she tightened her fingers around the pole, anticipating the burn that always followed.

She'd forgotten how much this hurt but there was nothing she could do about it.

Within a heartbeat of feeling the initial wriggle in her gut, she opened her mouth, allowing the flames the outlet they needed. Bright orange lit the darkness, scorching the sidewalk a deep black before it finally finished.

Swiping a hand across her mouth, she pushed off the lamp and tossed the bottle into the bushes. It thumped against something and she grunted. "Damn alcohol."

Ignoring the smell of melting concrete, she weaved away, trying not to think about Byron Kelly the IV.

Stupid, egotistical, pain in her ass, Byron Kelly IV.

Kicking the tire of the car she was passing, helped, but annoyed her even more when the thing folded in on itself and popped loudly, setting off the vehicle's alarm.

A man's bellow echoed into the night from one of the nearby row homes. "Ya bloody wench! What be ye about out there?"

"Sorry!" she yelled back. It came out more like *Sworry*, but he apparently got it when the alarm went off and a door slammed.

"Stupid men." She snickered drunkenly, bent enough to pat the poor, deflated tire before continuing on.

Getting her bearings, she turned left at the next intersection. Grams and Gramps home was just a few blocks away and hopefully she could make it without further incident. Or damage to personal property.

35

There were times she hated her life. She really did. Tonight was one.

Could *she* help it that she'd always been slightly stronger than your average girl?

No, she couldn't. It was part and parcel to The Curse, as she'd come to call it.

Could she help it, if on the occasion she was upset or depressed or, yes even drunk, she belched fire?

No, she couldn't. Again, it was part and parcel to her 'condition', as her folks liked to call the mess that was her life.

It was one of the reasons she'd become a computer programmer. Being able to work mostly from home, on her own, meant she didn't have to expose others to her freakishness. Except on rare occasions anyway.

It was on one such that she'd met Byron. He was handsome and charming and attentive and all the things her naïve heart had thought made up the perfect man...

But Byron wasn't perfect. Far from it actually and it wasn't until they'd moved in together that she found out just how imperfect he was.

"Oh well, he's done," she muttered around a fire-laden hiccup.

Yes, he was done, gone and no, wait, she'd left.

Which is how she'd found herself in Edinburgh, on a dark night, staggering down the street toward the only place she'd consider a refuge.

Grams and Gramps.

Stumbling up the steps, she was surprised to see a light on in the living room.

Had she called them? She couldn't honestly

remember much after getting off the plane, so she might have.

The digital numbers on her watch were blurry but she managed to make out the time. Just after 4 a.m.

Crap and double crap.

If she *had* called them, she was in for an earful. If she hadn't, well, she'd probably still get a dressing down for bumbling in drunk as a skunk.

It took five tries to get the key in the lock, but it finally twisted open...from the other side. Jumping back and biting down on a yelp, she lifted her fuzzy vision toward the shadow blocking the doorway.

"Gramps?"

He certainly didn't look like her grandfather, but it was hard to tell between the alcohol hampered fog in her brain and the darkness encompassing him.

And the deep resonate voice that replied *certainly* wasn't Gramps. "No. I am not your Grandpare."

She staggered back and the heel of her boot caught on the lip of the top step. Balance became an issue and she wind milled her arms to keep from tumbling back down to the street.

The shadow moved, stepping into the porch light and a long-fingered hand shot out, enveloping her wrist in a firm grip.

She hung there, half on the top step, half in the air and sucked in a hard breath as she took in his face.

A high-brow led to a long nose with several crooks across the bridge, as if it had been broken a couple of times. Strong cheeks led to beautifully full lips and down to a firm jaw. A slight cleft in the middle of his chin pointed down to a perfect neck and she found herself utterly fascinated by the pulse thrumping

37

ferociously at its base.

And then he changed.

Literally.

Before her intoxicated eyes, his human features morphed. It was the only way to describe it as the high-brow suddenly sprouted scales and spikes and his molten orange eyes darkened to a deep red. The hand around her wrist shifted into a talon-laden claw but when she looked up again, he was back to being human.

Mostly at least.

His eyes still blazed that fire-engine red and his lips parted on a sigh and then a half-smile. And when he spoke, his voice did all sorts of things to the heat in her belly, mainly threatening to explode it from her body and burn her from the inside out.

"Hello *Kyleri*, it is nice to finally meet you."

***

Fallon's head was going to explode. It was that simple. It was going to burst open and leak her brain all over...

Cracking an eye she recognized the fuzzy outline of red and blue flowers on the pillowcase of Grams spare bed.

"Would you like some Soya root, *Kyleri*?"

A deep male voice reverberated through her cotton-clogged grey matter and she blinked, seeking out the owner.

He, whoever he was, leaned against the window, arms folded over the blurred outline of his chest. Daylight streaming through the glass cast the rest of him in shadow, except for his eyes, which were bright orange.

"Would I like, what?" is what she wanted to say, but what came out was, "Huh?"

He pushed off and strolled across the room. As the shadows cloaking him dissipated, she got her second good look and couldn't remember to breathe. His strong face had a relaxed but self-assured quality to it, like nothing would ever come near her again. His smoky hair was long in front and he swiped the strands back as he sat on the bed. He gently nudged the hair off her face. "Would you like some Soya root?" he asked again. "I brought some with me."

She sucked air into her lungs when heat flamed across her skin and shrunk into the pillows. Swallowing the thickness on her tongue, she found her voice, or tried too. "Who, are you?"

One side of his mouth slowly cocked up, showing a dimple in his left cheek and she had an undeniable urge to lick it. "I am Fyris."

The introduction came out in such a way that he seemed to expect her to know exactly who he was. Which she didn't and was pondering that when a pounding on the front door thundered through her hangover. It sounded twice more then stopped. She could just make out Gramps voice down the hall then Byron's echoed across the house.

"Fallon! Get out here woman! I know you're here!"

Fyris' head swung toward it. It came back around and his brow pinched. "You know this person?"

She gulped, working some salvia into her mouth, easing out from under the covers. "Unfortunately. Excuse me."

Yanking open the door, she answered his bellow

39

with one of her own, even though it caused her head to ache all the more. "What?"

Her former boyfriends heavy feet came around the stairs and the look on his face didn't bode well at all. Lines creased his forehead and his green eyes spit fire and brimstone the second he spotted her. "Get out here, right now." He snapped his fingers, like she was some sort of dog. "We're going home."

Why she'd ever thought he was handsome was beyond her, but she had, and now here he was, come to retrieve her like some errant child. "I don't think so," she muttered. "Get out. We're done."

He took four steps and wrapped her upper arm in a fierce grip, fingers digging into her flesh. "No one leaves a Kelly. Now, come. I have the jet waiting."

She planted her feet, the fire in her belly ready to erupt. She couldn't though, not here. She didn't want to burn down Grams house. "No!" She yanked back against his hand, wrapping her free one around the door jamb. "We're done, Byron."

He spun, bringing a fist around to crack her across the cheek. He was swinging it back the other way when a hand shot over her shoulder and caught it mid-swing.

She recognized the rippling forearm with its coating of smoky hair and gulped, waiting to hear something break. She wasn't disappointed. Without a word, the fingers tightened and both bones in his forearm snapped.

Byron howled and staggered away, cradling the appendage against his chest. "Who, the hell, are you?" he managed between cries.

She didn't give Fyris a chance to answer. Shoving Kelly in the chest, she guided him to the door and kicked him in the ass for good measure when he stumbled over the threshold. "Don't come back," she managed around the pounding in her head. "Ever."

She slammed it in his wake and sank back against it.

Fyris stood at the base of the stairs, arms crossed and fingers tapping against the opposite arm.

She quirked an eyebrow. "What?"

His demeanor had changed. Gone was the self-assured look. In its place was something all-together terrifying. The orange of his eyes blazed bright red and black streaks swirled through the irises. The pulse in his neck flickered rapidly, his breathing was deep and grey smoke coiled out of his nostrils on every exaltation. He sort of looked like that bull she'd seen in the cartoons she streamed on her monitors whenever she was bored.

"Move *Kyleri*," he growled.

She blinked at him. "What?"

"I was not finished. Move."

There was a command in there she instinctively wanted to follow. But reason won out and she slowly shook her head. "No. He won't be back."

He didn't look at all convinced. Wrapping his long fingers around her waist, he lifted her like she weighed nothing and set her to the side.

Which wasn't an easy feat in and of itself. Being a computer programmer, she'd become lazy in the last years and it showed around her middle. She hated the fact that she'd put on some extra weight, but just didn't have the gumption to do anything about it. There was always some project or the next hack or some other thing to distract her from exercise.

Not that she was proud of it, it just was.

She wasn't unhealthy, just fluffy. But that didn't seem to be an issue for this man.

He cupped a hand around her neck and his thumb stroked along her jaw. For a heartbeat, the red faded from his eyes, replaced with a soft orange and he smiled. "I know he will not be back. I will see to it."

He turned for the door and that same instinct kicked in. Grabbing his arm, she planted a foot against the wall. "Oh no you don't. Let it go. He's gone." Her voice had a slight pleading in it she wasn't sure she liked or not. "You don't need to defend me."

The muscles under her fingers rippled and his other hand paused on the doorknob. He cut a look over his shoulder, that red blazing through his eyes again as they dropped to the throbbing bruise on her cheek. They slid to the darkening marks on her arm and clouded over. "He harmed you. It will not happen again."

His hand twisted on the knob and pulled open the door.

Slamming her other foot against it, she managed to kick it shut again. "Gramps!"

Her Grandpa came down the hallway on the other side of the stairs, a bagel in one hand and coffee in the other. His still bright silver eyes took in the scene and he shook his head. Setting the cup and half-eaten pastry on the steps, he sighed. "Gone all Dragon on ya, has he lass?"

She grunted, throwing her weight into her grip to hold Fyris in place as best she could. "I don't know what he's doing. Other than trying to get out the door and kill my Ex!"

The man she'd spent many a Saturday being

regaled by his tales of legends and myths, chuckled. With a meaty hand, he spun Fyris around and a haymaker out of somewhere in Florida followed, nailing him dead-center on the chin.

The poor guy dropped like a sack of taters, out cold and she landed on her own considerable backside with an oomph. She looked up at the man she'd always trusted and snorted. "What the hell was that?"

Tom Heegan squatted down, his gaze rolling from her to Fyris and back again, his dancing silver eyes amused. "Lass, he is a Dragon and from this reaction," he jerked a thumb at the man in question. "I would say he thinks you are his Mate."

Chapter Five

Bryon Kelly IV slapped the pain patch over his arm as the limo pulled away from the curb.

"Where to, Sir?" his driver asked.

"Find me the nearest Police Station," he growled. He pressed the button to raise the partition between them and lifted the vid-glasses off the hook by the door. "Home office," he said into the mic.

The connection between Edinburgh and Denver, Colorado established with a crack and he blinked through the menu on the screen until it dialed his father's private number.

Byron Kelly III's deep voice snapped in his ear. "Did you get her?"

"No," he bit back. "I was too late."

His father's glaring face spiraled into view on the small right screen. "What do you mean too late?"

He shook in fear that had nothing to do with the discomfort in his arm. "A Dragon was already here."

The other side of the vid-glasses filled with a long, black face. A red eye bore into his across the vast distance and the golden horn sprouting out its forehead glittered in the artificial lighting of his father's office. "Then kill it and bring her anyway."

He gulped, wishing the injection of drugs from the patch would work faster. "Yes Master Golix," he muttered. "Right away."

***

Golix paced the wide, opulent penthouse of his new company, Blackhorn, Inc.

"He will get the job done."

He turned toward the human, snapping a hoof against the hardwood flooring. "He had better." He strode to the desk, leaning over it to catch the man's eye. "You two had one job. Just one. Keep the woman under control until I arrived."

Byron Kelly III gulped and nodded slowly. "I know. My son,"

He cut the man off. "Had better not ruin my plans." He pulled back, staring down his long snout. "If he has, I will make you watch when I flay him alive. Do you understand?"

Kelly Sr. ducked his greying head. "I do, Master. Please, I know my son can be a handful, but he is a good boy."

He huffed out a cloud of smoke. "You had better hope so."

"Yes, Master."

He walked away and back to his own office off the penthouse. He'd decided to operate from here instead of in the main suite out of habit, preferring to remain anonymous as always. Crossing into the room, he stared at the bank of monitors and the short, gangly boy sitting in front of several keyboards. On the screens, the human world scrolled along, oblivious he was among them and poised to put his plans into action.

"Where are we?"

The boy turned a bit, smiling sidelong to expose yellowed, cracked teeth. His pointed nose reminded him of some of the Satyr's back home and his slightly pointed ears barely held his stringy, greasy looking hair out of his eyes. "Everything is ready Boss. I just need that bitch to crack the final coding. Once she has, I can jack in the six algorithms and hack the main network."

"Excellent. I need one final thing."

One of Mallice's black eyes sparkled. "Yeah? What's that?"

"A kill squad."

"A who what?"

He rolled his eyes. "Do you have no one in this world that will do your bidding for money?"

A grin spread across the boy's features. "Oh, you mean Merc's." He spun back to the keyboards, fingers flying across the surfaces. "Sure. I can find you someone. Give me..." He tapped for a moment then pointed at one of the screens. "There. A crew in Italy is open."

He narrowed a look at the information. "How far is that from this Edinburgh?"

Another cocky grin. "Just a simple plane ride. Totally doable. Shall I hire them?"

He debated a heartbeat then nodded. "Indeed."

"And the target?"

"One Dragon and two humans."

Mallice snickered. "Are you serious?" He cut another look over his shoulder. "Of course you're serious. You're a unicorn. What was I thinking..."

He almost knocked the insolent fool out of his chair and crushed his skull under a hoof. Much as it grated on his nerves, he needed the child, so he let it go. For now. But the day would come and he looked forward to the crunch of bone and spray of blood...

***

Byron Kelly IV sat in the limo, watching the street

and waiting. It was only a matter of time now. He'd made his report to the local police, who in this time of so little crime, practically foamed at the mouth for a *real* case. They'd gleefully recorded every word of his assault and nearly bowled him over getting out of their small station to head off and arrest the perpetrator.

With most crimes now either in the cyber world or nothing more than a neighborly dispute, the poor bastards had become almost obsolete.

But not today...

Like clockwork, they rolled up to the Heegan residence, sirens blaring and tires squealing. Jumping from their vehicles they bolted for the door, lazpistols drawn and ready for action.

He could almost smell their joy from here.

The first leapt the three steps and pounded on the door.

He cracked the window enough to hear the authoritative bellow.

"Police! We demand entry!"

He smiled. Oh yes, this was going to be perfect.

The front door opened in response and the officers pushed by the older man who'd answered his own knock earlier that morning. The door closed again but not for long.

It only took them a few minutes to appear again, dragging the bastard who'd broken his arm between them. All but stuffing him in one of the cars, they smiled widely, patting one another on the back, no doubt for a textbook arrest that was probably the first for either of them.

Fallon appeared on the porch, shaking a fist then whirled back into the house. The door slammed behind her and his smile widened as the two cars drove off.

"To the airport, Sir?"

"Not yet."

Fallon would go after them. It was just her way. She was a fixer, especially if she thought something was her fault.

He could hear her thinking now. If she hadn't come to Edinburgh, *he* wouldn't have had to chase after her and gotten hurt by that behemoth.

She loved him, he never doubted that. She'd only come here because he'd frightened her. He hadn't meant too, really he hadn't. But, the temper he'd kept in check for so long finally had enough of her sniveling and gotten the better of him two nights ago.

He knew the moment he'd hit her, he'd pushed the limit.

In his defense, if she hadn't snapped at him over some such thing or another, it wouldn't have happened. If she'd had dinner on the table like she was supposed to, like he'd told her she must do when they moved in together, he wouldn't have felt the need to teach her better.

The front door opened again and sure enough, out she came, that damned scruffy courier pouch over her shoulder. That had been what really set him off. If she'd just get rid of the thing, he would be happy. It was ancient, a sickly pea-green color and ragged at every corner. Patches covered every inch of it, though where they'd come from he had no clue.

Fallon never traveled, but apparently the bag had at some point and it was never far from her hand.

She paused now at the base of the steps then turned up the street, head down and a glare in her eye.

48

She was probably upset that she had to come find him. She'd plead with him to take her back and he would. He'd let her beg first, of course, maybe even grovel and crawl some. She needed to learn, it was that simple.

"Get her."

The driver's door opened and Jackson got out, towering over the vehicle. He jogged across the street and he watched them talking.

Ok, it wasn't really talking.

Jackson stopped in front of her and said something he couldn't hear.

Fallon's shoulders drew back and she tried to step around him.

His driver's fist shot out and caught dead in the chin.

She crumpled. Scooping her up, he carried her back to the limo and deposited her on the back seat.

"Was that really necessary?" he asked when the man folded himself behind the wheel.

"She was not going to come peacefully, Sir. I had to, take steps."

He glared toward the front seat. "You'd best hope you didn't break something."

"I did not."

He checked Fallon over and sighed softly, shifting her dark red hair off her face. Even though she weighed a good 50 lbs. more than he usually liked, she was still pretty in her own way.

Not marrying pretty, but passable for a fling.

He got comfortable as the limo headed for the airport. By evening they'd be back in Denver and he could hand her over to The Master.

When she'd done whatever it was they wanted her to do, she'd be all his...again. And this time, he'd make sure she had no way to leave him, ever.

***

"And I have told you. I did not assault anyone. I merely defended my *Kyleri*."

Officer Kendall's blue eyes narrowed into slits. "And what is that again?"

Fyris rolled his and leaned back in the chair. They'd been asking him the same questions over and over and over again for most of the daylight and he'd swear humans were even more stupid than he'd been lead to believe. "She is my mate."

"So, now you're saying you're married to Fallon Heegan?"

"I do not know what that words means. But we are Mates, yes."

Kendall sat forward a bit, tapping on the small screen inset into the table. "Let's start this again. Tell me what happened."

So he did. He explained, again, how the human had burst into the house, demanded his *Kyleri* go with him and then hit her first. He'd intervened before it happened again. Beyond that things were a little blurred in his memory and he could only assume he'd gone into a Blood Rage.

Kendall propped a hand under his chin, his face a blank, unreadable slate. Which again, confirmed his thoughts that humans were not so smart. "So, you're trying to say that Byron Kelly IV, from one of *the* most respected families on the planet, hit a poor defenseless

50

woman?"

He didn't like the way that was phrased. At all. And was on the verge of asking, when the door opened.

The other authority figure that had been at the house to arrest him held it open. "Let him go."

Kendall blinked, finally showing some signs of life. "What?"

The second one shrugged. "The charges were dropped."

Kendall shook his head and tapped the screen again. "Looks like it's your lucky day. You're free to go."

Of course he was. He hadn't done anything. Well, at least not where he came from. Back home, defense of ones *Kyleri* was perfectly justified. Obviously not in the human world. Rising, he nodded in respect to the two officers and walked out of the room.

This didn't make any sense but he wasn't about to look a gift goblin in the mouth either. Exiting the building a heartbeat or so later, he paused on the street, unsure where he was in relation to Tom and Diana's home.

All he'd seen of the city thus far was the ride from the airport to their address, which Terra had provided him with before he left. He could shift into his true self and try to find it from the air, but Terra had warned him his magic probably wouldn't work here. He had yet to try it to know for sure...

It was solved for him, however, when a vehicle pulled up and the couple emerged.

Tom smiled and dropped an arm around Diana's shoulders. "Ah, excellent. See you are already out."

He lifted an eyebrow. "Yes, I am. But, I do not understand why they let me go after so long. They seemed rather intent on me staying there."

Diana laughed and patted his chest. "My granddaughter is not the only one with computer skills son."

That didn't make a lick of sense either. But, if it got him out of that horrid little room, with its horrid little humans, who was he to question.

Tom's gaze roamed the street. "Where is Fallon? She still inside?"

Blood rushed into his ears and his hearts pulsated a triple beat. "She is not with you?"

Diana's face went ghostly white. "No, she left hours ago to come after..."

"Byron," they both said at the same time.

"Dammit all to hell and back," Tom cursed. He checked the timepiece on his wrist, reaching for the door handle at the same time. "They have at least six hours on us. We might be able to..."

He wasn't all that familiar with the human world, but human or draconic, some things remained the same. And a black van rolling way too slowly down the street was a premonition of bad things to come, especially when the scales on the back of his neck rose.

"Down!"

Tom spun and took Diana down with him at the same time he dove for the ground himself. And not a hearts beat too soon either as a hail of something pelted the car from the other side.

"What the hell?" Tom asked when the barrage ended.

He scrambled close to the vehicle and peeked around the end, spying the four humans forming a semi-circle around the van. They were doing something with the weapons in their hands and he ducked back. "Again!" he bellowed.

The car rocked against them with the second salvo.

"That, is, it! No one shoots at me!"

Diana squirmed out from under her husband and despite her aged appearance, grasped the edge of the vehicle. "Dear? Do you mind?"

He figured her intent and joined her. Folding his hands around the flimsy metal, he nodded and between them, they upended auto onto its side.

Diana grinned and winked. "Give her a shove dearest."

He laughed and gleefully put action to her request. He may not have the magic inherent to his kind in this world, but he still had the strength he was born with.

With a grunt, the machine rocketed away and the men that had been firing on them screamed when it crushed them against the van.

"I am going to guess this was Golix's doing?" Diana asked.

He sighed. "I would have to say yes."

Tom crossed his arms, his brows pinching together. "Which means Kelly must work for him. Otherwise how would he know you're here?"

He scrubbed a hand down his face then through his hair. This daylight just got a whole lot worse. "Where would this human take Fallon?"

"Back home I suppose," Diana replied.

"Which is where?"

"Denver, Colorado."

His hearts ached and fear coiled through his gut.

Golix was definitely involved. He had to be. This Denver city was the exact place Terra had recognized in the portal and where she'd told him to start. And *if* Golix had Fallon, there was no telling what he was truly up too or what he might put her through to reach his goals...

Chapter Six

"So, how is it the two of you are still alive?" Fyris asked as they waited for the plane to taxi for take-off.

Diana snuggled down into her husband's side and smiled across the small aisle. "As you know Dragons are long-lived and I just so happen to know a thing or two about blood magic." She turned a loving look up at Tom, or Thorak as he'd once been known. "When I decided I wanted this man in my life for as long as possible, I cast a spell to slow his aging process."

Tom smiled down at her. "Worst thousand years of my life, lad, let me tell ya," he whispered affectionately.

Despite the years, he'd never lost his heavy Scottish brogue and even though the comment sounded derisive, the look in his eyes was anything but.

Diana laughed and elbowed him in the ribs before her gaze swung back to him. "Don't let him fool you, he's loved every minute of it."

He smiled in return and asked another question, more for curiosities sake than anything else. "And how have you kept your true nature hidden from the humans?"

Diana threw back her head and laughed. "Now that was a far sight more difficult. Especially now. With them able to communicate at the click of a mouse, it's been a chore to hide ourselves, but we've managed. It's mostly involved a string of identities and the help of family."

"But Terra and Lanni did not know until they saw your departure from the Kingdoms in a vision. Why?"

Diana shrugged one shoulder. "We thought it best to keep our distance from most of the family. But, every generation we pick one branch and become their grandparents."

"Would lend credence to your claim of being human."

Diana tapped the end of her nose. "Exactly."

"And how is Fallon related? Is she sister to Terra and Lanni?"

Tom answered this time. "Goodness no. She is an indirect cousin. Her mother is also of Decia's blood line."

Dragon linage worked much the same, more or less. His kind rarely had true children. Most females came into a breed cycle once every 200 Suns and the chance they'd be mated at the time was small. If they conceived, it was usually for convenience and nothing more. Once they had, they retreated high into the Northern Snows and laid their egg, or if they were truly lucky in the case of his younger siblings, eggs in the favored nesting grounds. After that, the mother hibernated atop it until it hatched sometime the following Sun.

He and Draven's mother, an unusual pair of siblings in their own right, nested together 400+ years ago and he'd always considered the monarch more of a brother than just a mere nest mate.

Which was the sole reason he was on this crazy adventure...

He never expected, much less dreamed, he might find his own *Kyleri*, but there was no doubt in his mind, Fallon Heegan was exactly that. The night they'd met, despite her drunken state, she'd set his heart's pumping, his dick raging and had consumed his thoughts ever since. On some level he wasn't sure if he was happy with this development or not. He'd spent so long alone, through no fault of his own, that he'd convinced himself it would always be that way.

"She is Dragon-Born, yes?" he finally asked, pulling himself out of his own thoughts.

Tom chuckled. "Her mother is our great-granddaughter however many times removed."

Diana patted his knee. "I think we're on generation 12 or something now, dear." She smiled at him again. "My blood is thicker in her than most of the others from my line, though I honestly have no idea why. She's stronger than the average human and has a tendency to breathe fire when she's upset."

"Does she know what she truly is?"

Tom shook his head. "Oh no. We kept that a secret, just like we promised we would. But she does know she is different and quite frankly, the poor lass hates herself for it most days."

He fingered the long, ragged scar on his cheek and sighed, knowing that feeling all too well. He stayed silent after that, twisting things around in his mind as the plane took off, shot nearly straight up into the lower atmosphere and then began an almost immediate descent.

According to Terra, who had prepared him for her world as best she could, humans had cut their flight times down considerably. Where it had once taken them nearly an entire daylight to traverse the distance between continents, it now only took a few of their hours.

It still took his people more than a few daylights to get from one to the other, but here, as his stomach lurched into his throat from the change in altitude, they'd be back in this United States area by darkfall.

Which amazed and frankly impressed him...

Humans weren't much, but their level of technology was vastly superior to the Five Kingdoms. He made a mental note to gather as much information as possible before he returned home and left it at that.

Stretching back in the seat, he waited, trying not to worry over Fallon and whatever Golix might be doing to her, or had planned for her. Having witnessed what the bastard was capable of, he was anxious to come to her rescue.

Which shouldn't be the case, not really, but his instincts screamed at him to be at her side no matter what. Draven had said he'd felt much the same when he'd first met Terra, so it would follow for him too. Wouldn't it?

It shouldn't, they were strangers after all, but it did.

Acid broiled through his gut at the thought of her in Golix's clutches for even the day it would take them to get there.

Fear and worry tingled along his nerves at what she might be going through in that very moment.

Dread knocked his hearts together at the thought of even a hair on her head being harmed by the evil Unicorn.

And finally rage threatened to overwhelm him at what *he* would do if *any* of those same scenarios had indeed happened...

The wheels screeching against the tarmac jarred him back to reality and he blinked across the way at Terra and Lanni's grandparentals as they too stirred.

"Evening folks. Welcome to Denver, Colorado," the

pilot's disembodied voice said. "*The tower has informed me there is a car waiting to take you where you need to go...*"

***

Golix watched the two Dragons and the human disembark from the private jet they'd chartered in Edinburgh with a dissatisfied grunt. Hitting the back of the Mallice's chair with a hoof, he gave the only order he could. "Make sure the troops know what to do."

The kid grinned, his black eyes gleaming wickedly. "You got it, Boss. Should I bring the bitch up to watch the fun or not?"

He turned toward the monitor to find Fallon sitting quietly in the corner of the room where Byron had put her when they arrived earlier that morning. "No, not yet. Make sure they are alive for leverage."

Mallice nodded and turned toward his precious keyboards, tapping out his commands. One of the screens flashed to an outside view and several others to interior shots where the troops he paid all too well were getting ready.

This would be so much easier if he had his magic!

But, he didn't and had to rely on the humans to do his bidding. Which had its advantages, mainly for the fact *if* things went awry, he could always escape back to The Kingdoms and try again. The humans, more specifically the Kelly family, would take the fall with the authorities here, not him.

Because, what logical human would believe a *Unicorn* was behind everything. Not many. According to them, *he* only existed in myths and fairy tales. And that played right into his plans...

"Here they come, Boss."

He blinked out of his thoughts and focused on the screens.

A car rolled up in front of the building and the three got out. They stood for a moment on the sidewalk, talking and he kicked the back of Mallice's chair again. "Sound!"

The child winced and tapped.

"Are you sure about this?" the older woman asked.

The younger dragon, one of the Taraxus line, nodded, his eyes pinching against the setting sun. "If she is in there, I have to try."

The older human male crossed his arms, shaking his head. "It is a trap," he said in a thick accent.

The dragon turned back to them. "Then go. I will not put you two in danger."

The woman looked up at the older man and sighed. "She is our granddaughter. We all go..."

He laughed. Oh yes, everything was going just like he wanted it too. He knew hiring the kill squad would send them running after the human girl. Another step in his overall plan to bring everything he needed to one spot.

Mallice cackled as the three strode into the lobby. "They'll never see it coming, Boss."

The images switched to the interior view and they both laughed a second time as the two dragons and the human were surrounded.

They tried to resist and he could admit to a moment of worry when it looked like it might swing their way, but he shouldn't have.

The men the Kelly's employed were the best and

but one of the reasons he'd chosen the family as his patsy's. That and their significant income...

The first wave of troops went down and it was the second, firing the halothane gas into the trio that brought them down.

He watched them carried off to the holding rooms he'd made ready when they'd found the chartered flight from Edinburgh.

"Get the girl."

Mallice clapped his hands together and headed off to do his bidding. He returned moments later, dragging Fallon along by the upper arm.

"Let go of me you piece of shit!"

He turned toward the angry outburst and introduced himself. "Hello Ms. Heegan, I am Golix and I bid you welcome."

She stopped dead, swinging her eyes up and down him in a slow sweep of silver that reminded him of two other humans. For just a moment there was a brief flicker of disbelief and then she did the most unexpected thing.

She laughed.

And it was not a mildly amused sort of chuckle but a full out guffaw that grated on every nerve he had.

Bending over, she clutched her sides and then sat heavily on the floor, kicking her feet as she continued to giggle uncontrollably.

Mallice turned a bright red and he almost swore there was steam bubbling up from under the collar of his t-shirt as he reached down and jerked her back to her feet. "Show some respect to the Boss Man there bitch!"

Fallon looked like she was trying to get herself

under control but every time her eyes swung his way, the giggles started all over again. When she could, she managed a few words. "You can't be serious!" She turned toward her fellow hacker, pointing at him as she added, "Mallice, is this one of your holograms?"

The younger man pulled his shoulders back, sniffing in disdain. "Not even close. This is Golix, the Master…"

His comment only started her laughing again and she was once more on the floor, rolling from side to side as her amusement consumed her.

He cracked a hoof. "Enough!"

She sobered, somewhat, and sat up, cutting Mallice yet another look of disbelief. "Really dude? A Unicorn? That was the best you could do?"

He turned toward the hacker, awaiting an explanation.

Mallice shifted from one foot to the other. "She and I have this thing," he said, a nervous hitch to his voice. "We try to outdo each other's holograms."

He strode forward and bent down until his good eye was level with hers. "I assure you Ms. Heegan, I am quite real."

She sputtered out another chuckle and reached out a hand.

He wasn't sure of her intent, but knocked it aside with his horn.

She looked at the appendage then back up at him before scurrying backwards, stopping only when her back thumped into the wall. "You're, you're real!"

He took four steps and put a hoof on her chest, pressing her back further. "I am. Now, are you going to do as I say, or do things need to get, unpleasant…"

She gulped, hard. "What, what do you want?"

He smiled and moved his hoof. "It is quite simple really." He jerked a nod toward the monitors and keyboards. "You will crack the code for the Centralized Reserve."

Her eyes went wide. "That's, illegal. I won't do it."

He bent enough to pin her with his good eye again. "Show her."

Mallice's fingers clacked on the keys.

Fallon swung a look that direction and she sucked in a hard breath. "What?!"

He explained calmly. "You will or you can watch them die one by one…"

Chapter Seven

Tyleios Cannis willed the communication stone to activate. There was so much to say to The Master and he needed some direction as well. As if on cue, the circular device beeped twice and cracked, spitting out a cloud of blue smoke before Golix's face appeared.

Cannis had no clue what he might have done on his side of things to strengthen the connection, but whatever it was, it worked.

Golix's face spiraled into view and his strong voice echoed through the Throne Room. "Where are we?"

He cleared his throat. "Bra'ka is still ours. There has been no sign of further attack from Draven and his lot. The shield is holding, Master. For now."

"You have not found the human then?"

"Not as of yet, Sire," he replied, adding quickly, "But we did catch Turosh skulking around the Shi-so last darkfall."

"Where is that half-ogre now?" Golix growled.

"Being questioned as we speak. If anyone knows where the Heegan woman is, he will," Cannis blurted out. "We will find her."

Golix's remaining eye narrowed. "You had better. If the spell is not completed, the shield will eventually fail."

He gulped. "I know, Master. We have been using the citizens in the interim, but they do not last. Two rotations has been the longest so far."

The Master's long face nodded. "Then put in more than one. You must keep the energy stream active at all times."

He bowed his head. "Yes Master."

"And what of Carax?" he asked next, switching subjects quickly.

"He left just this daylight. He should arrive in Rosau by darkfall after next and then plans to move on to Gahroon," Cannis returned calmly.

Golix's eyebrow slowly rose. "What was the delay?"

He gulped nervously, hating this bit of news. The Master never liked bad news. "We had to refit several of the ships that were damaged and reset four of the devices he will use in his attack on Rosau."

The eyebrow slipped higher and he explained hastily. "Seems there is a saboteur in the ranks, Master. He or she was able to override the timers on several of the bombs you had built for this stage of your plan. It took considerable effort..."

Golix snorted softly and he could almost feel the heat of his anger on the back of his neck even though they were literally worlds apart. "I do not care how much effort you put into fixing your mistake, Tyleios. Did you get it done?"

He dropped his eyes to the floor. "Yes, Master, we did. When Carax arrives in Chimera's port city, I have no doubt the devices will wipe the citizens out with little or no damage..."

***

Carax paced the bow of the *N'Val*.

How dare his father delegate such a menial task to him!

He snorted and pawed the deck. Bombing a city

wasn't even close to being worthy of his place in The Herd or as Golix's son. Never mind that he was a bastard, in the traditional sense, because his parents had never mated. His Grandmare wouldn't allow it, that bitch. Good thing she was dead now, or he might have had to take matters under his own hoof at some point.

Neither here nor there.

Still, he should be running Bra'ka, not that misshapen son of a Goblin, Cannis! He should be on the throne, not sent off to the farthest regions of nowhere to handle a bunch of worthless Chimera.

It just wasn't fair.

One of the Orc's crewing the ship interrupted his internal tirade. "Sire? Would you care for a meal?"

He snorted and pawed the deck again, turning a look back over his flank. "No!" he snapped. "I want this mission done with. Put more wind in the sails!"

The Orc turned an unhealthy shade of green, darker than usual, but nodded and turned to shout the command back over his shoulder.

The material above billowed out with a hard snap and a heartbeat later, the *N'Val's* speed increased. The sooner he got this over with, the quicker he could return to Bra'ka and kill that imposter King...

***

"Land Ho!"

Carax jerked awake and smiled around a yawn. It was about time. The trip here seemed to take forever. Striding out of the bridge housing, he moved to the bow and watched the tiny dots of light making up Rosau slowly form into the small city. It was the only thing standing in the way of the Army under his command.

A rotation behind the *N'Val*, they would arrive and clean the village of the carcasses. After that, it would be theirs and no one would get past them. With it under their control, it was another step in his father's plans to rule it all!

His smile widened the closer they got. The ship under his hooves vibrated as the doors carved in bottom opened in preparation for the attack. He should go down there and make sure everything went off like it was supposed to, but he much preferred the view from up here.

He couldn't wait to hear the citizens scream and beg for mercy from their unseen attackers...

His flanks shivered in anticipation.

"All is ready Sire. Shall I give the order?" the ship's captain asked from behind him.

His grin widened a third time. "Indeed. Bombs away..."

***

Arin curled an arm tighter around Haydn. Pulling her back against his naked chest, he nuzzled into her long, blue hair with a contented sigh. Life was good. Despite the challenges still ahead, as long as she loved him...

Wait. Love?

When did that happen?

Somewhere around Bra'ka when she saved your life...again.

He chuckled, sighed a second time and let his thoughts drift. There were a hundred and one things he should be doing, they *both* should be doing, but for the life of him, he didn't want to move.

For just this one moment, the Universe wasn't against them.

There was no evil Unicorn bent on ruling anything he could get his grubby little hooves into.

There was no shield cutting them off from Bra'ka.

There was absolutely no need to go running off anywhere...

There *was* just the two of them.

A man and a woman, content to lay in each other's arms and let the world pass by.

Haydn snorted, mumbling in her sleep and he drew her closer, kissing the back of her head tenderly. "Shhh love, all is well."

He'd no sooner whispered the words than the door burst inward. And if he'd thought his little assassin was a heavy sleeper, he was quite wrong. The portal had barely come to a slamming halt against the wall and she was out of the bed, crouched in the corner, a sword in one hand, a small, fully loaded crossbow in the other.

She was completely naked, unconcerned with is and growled toward the intruder, her red-blue eyes bright and fully awake. "Who? What?"

He laughed outright, pushed up on an elbow and looked toward the interruption.

Draven stood on the threshold, his face shadowed and his chest heaving. "Arin," he managed around gulps of air.

He flopped the covers back, reaching for his pants with one hand and tossing Haydn hers with the other. "What? What is wrong?"

Draven drew in a long lungful of air. "It is Rosau. It

has been bombed."

***

Terra listened, yet again, to the sketchy report echoing out of the monitor.

"This is fourth guard Balc. Myself, Alpha Souda and a dozen or so of the Royal Court have managed to take refuge under the Usac. If anyone can hear this, please, we are under attack." A loud bang shook the small screen. *"Send reinforcements."* Balc coughed heavily. *"There are bombs dropping all over Rosau. They are leaking some form of gas..."*

The poor Chimera coughed again, harder this time then continued. *"We need help. It is killing us. The streets are full of bodies..."*

Static took the place of his voice and she tapped the keys to replay it, just as Draven returned with Arin and Haydn in tow.

They all listened and one of Haydn's hands slipped into hers and she saw the woman's other gripping Arin's forearm as Balc's desperate pleas filled the room.

The War Advisor's entire frame shook. "Any idea who might have done this?"

She reached over and stopped the recording and clicked on the small screen to play the first one she'd heard.

"This is Edeth Manus. Rosau is under attack," it began and Arin sucked air into his lungs. *"Please, send help..."*

"Arin," Haydn whispered.

She gripped her friend's hand. "That was the first one. Balc's came next and then there was one more, but it's pretty much the same. The last one said the bombs were coming from ships over the city."

Arin turned a look on Draven that no one had a problem understanding. "I have to go," he said much more calmly than she would have thought possible.

Draven nodded. "Of course my friend." He reached for a drawer and pulled out a communication stone, handing it over to the Chimera. "Let us know what you find."

Arin tucked it in his pocket and flicked worried eyes toward Haydn.

She said simply, "I will get the gear and meet you on the roof."

With that, they were both gone.

Draven waited a heartbeat and took a single step toward her, holding open his arms. "*Kyleri?*"

With a gulp, she folded into him, doing her best to stifle a sob. His reassuring hands roamed up and down her back and for a just a second or so, she managed to forget she was actually mad at him. Biting down on a knuckle, she spoke around it quietly. "How many live in Rosau?"

His deep sigh ruffled her hair. "About seventy-thousand Chimera, why?"

She bit down harder on her flesh. Dear Gods above. Seventy-thousand? And from the sounds of it, most of them were already dead. Who would do such a thing? And, more importantly, why?

"To control the port," Draven replied to her unspoken questions.

She nuzzled into his chest, hot tears pooling in her eyes. "Is it that important?"

His chin rubbed against the top of her head with

his nod. "It is the one of the few ways in and out of Dhar'go. Port Rilas on the southern tip is another, but it does not have the strategic importance or defensibility that Rosau does."

***

Arin's thick wings beat against the air, fear and something akin to panic driving him across the treetops. Haydn was perched on his back, her firm hands digging into his twin manes. Her long legs gripped around his shoulders and urged him through the darkfall.

It took them most of the dark to cross the jungle that encompassed and hid Win-ra from prying eyes and most of the daylight to reach the ragged cliffs surrounding the port city. He landed, almost in the exact spot he'd met Balc all those rotations ago.

For just a tick, his twin hearts knocked together at the pile of Tava bones that had been left by Dinsa oh so long ago but he managed to ignore them in the wake of this newest disaster.

"Down!" Haydn hissed as she slid from his back.

He shifted and flattened against the rocks, slithering forward just behind her toward the edge.

Below them, the city looked completely normal.

The buildings were all intact. Their windows gleamed brightly in the high daylight. Vehicles remained where they'd been parked the darkfall before. The ships that had been coming into to unload still bobbed against the waves in the harbor.

But there were no Chimera. This time of day, the streets should be teeming with citizens moving here and there on whatever business they were about. Even the Usac remained dark and unlit.

He gulped, hard and shifted his gaze to the building were Edeth had been attending classes. It too was empty, devoid of life and his hearts punched against one another in a rapid staccato beat. "Where, is everyone?"

Haydn's hand dropped into one of the bags of gear and pulled out a lorgnette. Spinning it open, she put it to her eye and slowly passed it from one side of Rosau to the other. She sucked in a long hiss of cold air and closed it up again.

He reached for it but she tucked it away. "No. My love, you do not want to see."

His voice broke, despite his efforts to keep it calm. "Yes, I need too."

She put a hand over his as he tried to dig the spyglass back out. "No, please. Just trust me. They are, dead."

Rage coiled through his gut, setting it on fire. "All of them?"

A tear pooled in Haydn's eye, sliding slowly down her cheek as she nodded. "All of them," she repeated on a low whisper.

Chapter Eight

The rage vibrated off Arin in a wave.

Haydn saw it, understood it and acted. Before he could rush off and do something utterly stupid!

Jumping on his back, she wrapped both arms around his neck and squeezed. Her lover struggled, grunting and growling, the long fingers that had just the night before stroked her skin so tenderly, dug into the rocky ground.

Fortunately for him, she wasn't a small woman and he couldn't gain enough purchase to get away. She hated to do this, but there wasn't another choice. He would have seen that if his eyes weren't filmed over with hate.

Not that she blamed him. If it had been her people down there, she'd feel much the same, despite her lack of empathy for her own race.

Waiting until he'd collapsed again, out cold, she sat up with a hard sigh. Feathering her fingers through his hair, she checked his breathing and dug a length of rope from the bags of gear. Binding his wrists and ankles, she paced off a few steps and stuffed her shaking hands into her pockets.

He would probably loath her, when he woke up again, but eventually he'd see reason. She hoped.

Digging out the spyglass, she hunkered down behind an outcropping of boulders and passed it over the buildings below.

As she'd told him, there was no movement, no people, just piles of bodies. She wasn't sure what had afflicted them in the darkfall, but whatever it was, acted fast. And silently.

She started from the beginning, trying to piece it together.

She found a crater, no doubt where one of the bombs had landed and expanded her search from there in a slow, deliberate circle. About half a block away, she found the first of the dead and tightened in on it. The equipment wasn't made for such distances, but she could get the gist of things with it.

Blood and some sort of white fluid had leaked from the eyes, nose and ears of the male Chimera. He lay on the payment, one hand clutched around the throat of the head on the left and the other stretching out to some unseen thing, as if he had been begging for aid.

She gulped, hard, not completely unaffected by the sight. Despite all her years of killing, it looked like a horribly way to go for sure. Moving on, she checked as many of Arin's kind as she could readily see and found most of them were the same.

One hand around a throat, another seeking help that never came...

Who in their right minds would do such a thing?

More importantly, why? What was to be gained from this genocide?

She could answer one of those questions easily enough. Golix. Or his minions had to be responsible. But again, the question became why?

Rosau had an advantage, sure. She knew enough to guess controlling the port would have importance to some sort of plan.

But why go this far? Why not just take the city and leave the occupants alive?

Surely having a ready pool of slave labor would be

better than wiping them out, wouldn't it?

Twisting it around from another angle, she gave this a once over from the reverse side of the equation. Why leave a pool of potential rebellion alive to, well, rebel. If they had the ability, which they clearly did, to clean out any and all resistance in one fell swoop, why not use it?

Closing up the glass again, she leaned a shoulder against the slab she'd taken refuge behind and sighed softly. She'd seen enough but that didn't stop her from trying to figure out what possible motive could be behind this.

She was still working on it when the distant rumble of an engine interrupted her. Whipping up the glass, she sought out the source and found the *N'Val*, hovering in the air over the harbor.

Two more ships sat behind it, all three waiting. She wasn't sure what they were doing until the crack of a sail punctuated the deathly silence that had fallen over the area. Shifting her view to the water, she spied a fleet of ships heading their way. From this distance though she couldn't make out much detail, but she didn't have to wait long.

The small armada sailed into the port and within a heartbeat of arriving, Ogre's, Orcs and Centaurs swarmed over the ships that had been waiting to dock. Splashes quickly followed as the flunkies of Golix and his kind dumped the now dead crew members over the sides and into watery graves they didn't deserve…

She watched, helpless, as the half dozen or so vessels were cleared of the dead and confiscated by the invaders.

Cheers for their spoils echoed up the rocky cliffs

and her grip around the tube tightened with a crack of knuckles as they moved into the village and began to do the same.

As the daylight passed toward the darkfall, she could only sit there and rage, much as Arin had done, over their casual treatment of the victims. Bit by bit they piled the former residents atop one another and lit them on fire for disposal.

It was a gruesome sight, one she was glad Arin wasn't awake to see...

***

Arin stirred about the time the sun was setting in the distance. He groaned, rolled onto his back and slowly sat up. Blinking confused eyes, he stretched at the ropes around his wrists and those same eyes sought her out.

"What? Why?"

She pushed off the rocks and moved over to him, kneeling next to his thigh. Gently brushing a lock of hair off his forehead, she smiled in the growing darkness. "I am sorry, my love. I had no choice."

His arms shifted behind his back. "Why?" he asked again.

She dropped her hand into her lap with a hard sigh. "You were about to do something that would only get you killed."

"I, I," he managed to stutter. "You can untie me now. I am fine."

She searched his gaze, saw the lie in the golden pools and slowly shook her head. "Not yet, lover. When you are calm and can see reason, yes, but not now."

He twisted around, trying to examine the city again, but she gripped his chin firmly. "No," she whispered.

The pyre's still burned below, lighting the area in a macabre scene of further death and destruction and she couldn't let him go through that. Not that she didn't think he could handle it, but why expose him to further grief and agony when she didn't have too. The army was no longer celebrating their victory. Intent on clearing the streets, they'd fallen silent, as if on some level they realized what they'd done.

Not that she cared. If she could have, she'd have spent the daylight killing every last one of them herself, but she didn't want to leave Arin alone. Not to mention, even *with* her considerable skill set, she was severely outnumbered. And she was no fool...

"I, I need to witness," he whispered, his voice cracking with emotion.

She swiped at the tears on his cheeks with a knuckle. "No. You do not. There is nothing either of us can do now." She cupped her hands around his face, stroking his cheeks, his lips, his brow. "If there was, I would have done it."

He gulped, the animosity in the glittering pools of his eyes slowly fading. He leaned forward, burying his face in her neck.

She rubbed her hands up and down his back, consoling him the best she could, even though there was absolutely nothing she could do or say that would make this any better. Nothing and that, quite frankly pissed her off. Feathering her fingers in his hair, she hummed softly, accepting the silent sobs that shook his shoulders.

77

As the twin moons rose, his tears ceased. Neither of them had moved and she checked the village below, thankful the fires had burned out. Death still hung on the breeze and she knew he smelled it, one couldn't help but.

He said nothing and neither did she.

Now was not a time for words, but for grief and she let him have it without judgment. Arin was one of the strongest men she knew and the fact that he'd chosen to cry on *her* shoulder was a testament to how much he trusted her.

With a twist, she untied the knot at his wrists and his arms folded around her, dragging her close. She didn't resist. Wrapping one of her own around his neck, she continued to soothe him with the other until he finally sighed and spoke.

"We need to let Draven know."

She nodded against his cheek. "Yes. You should head back to Win-ra. This is not something for a stone."

He pulled back, his glowing eyes full of suspicion at her choice of words. "*I* should head back?"

She tucked an errant strand of hair behind his ear, nodding again. "Yes, love. You."

His gaze pinched into a glare and his words came out on a growl. "What are you going to do?"

She chuckled and searched his face for a moment, knowing this was the only chance they had to gain an upper hand in this mess. "What I do best..."

His head began to slowly twist side to side and a myriad of emotions flittered across his face. "Oh no, no, no and to all the Nether Worlds, no!"

She put two fingers to his lips. "Yes love. We will

not have this chance again. It is the perfect opportunity for us to..."

His growling denial interrupted her. "No! Woman! No!"

She kissed him, mainly because it might be awhile before she could again. He continued to try and contradict her unspoken plan but eventually softened under her insistent lips. His arms tightened around her back, yanking her against his chest as if he wouldn't let her go do what she was planning to do.

She *should* have done it already, just left him here with a knife close at hand to free himself when he woke. But, if she had, he'd just come after her. Of that she had no doubt. No, it was better this way, gaining his concurrence to her idea first. He wasn't going to like it, that much was clear, but he would see the reason of it.

Pressing him back on the rocks, she straddled his hips, rubbing her own against him. Despite the angry growl that emanated from his chest, his body betrayed him.

"Damn you Haydn," he bit out, his voice muffled against her neck. "Do not do this!"

She pulled back enough to see his eyes. "I must. I am the only one who can, Arin. You know this."

***

"She did *what*?!"

Arin grunted at Terra's outrage, the same feeling all but consuming him. "She has infiltrated Golix's minions."

The soon-to-be Queen paced the length and width of the small living area, kicking over the coffee table.

"*Kyleri*," Draven tried to calm her. "From the sounds of things, it was the only way."

She turned that ire on him and he was thankful to be out of the crosshairs, if but for a moment or two. "Don't you dare, stay out of this!"

Draven held up his hands and gave him a pitying look.

He could understand that. He wasn't exactly thrilled the woman he loved had gone off on some half-cocked fool-hardy plan either. But, after their lovemaking, she'd convinced him it was a feasible option.

She was an Orc. The majority of Golix's forces were Orcs. And even though her kind barely numbered in the thousands, they didn't all know one another. The likelihood that those occupying Rosau would recognize her was about as remote as they could get. And probably the only opportunity they would have to gain an insider's perspective. The potential information and insight into Golix's plans she could gather, was too great to pass up.

He'd already explained this to Terra, but she wasn't having it. "I am getting sick and tired of people doing things without asking me first!"

He chuckled softly. "It was not exactly as if we had a lot of time to consult you."

She snorted and threw a vase at his head.

He caught it and carefully set the fragile object on an end table. "I am sorry, My Queen," he said, catching a second before it could crash into the wall. "Haydn did not see another option. And neither did I."

With a scream, she spun on a heel and stomped out of their suite. Draven started after her but he wrapped a hand around his friend's arm to draw him up. "No, this is my fault. I will go."

His liege nodded and sighed. "Just try not to anger her further, yes? I have just begun to regain her trust."

He sighed and patted Draven on the shoulder. "I will do my best."

He left their suite, heading for the roof of the tree they'd been residing in. But, she wasn't there. Sniffing, he caught the scent of her displeasure, shifted and followed it. He didn't have to go far and found her large dragon self, coiled around one of the massive trees on the outskirts of the Harpy capitol. Her scales pulsed through every color of the rainbow. Red, green, orange, blue, red again, and orange as she chomped on a limb. She growled, muttering a long string of not so pleasant curses around the bark. "The nerve! The gall! The unmitigated balls of that woman!"

He landed on one of the thicker branches and waited it out. When there was a break in her tirade, he spoke, letting his own anger over this turn of events come through. "I am not happy with her decision either, Terra."

She cracked the branch in two, ignoring the half heading for the ground. "Then why didn't you stop her," she grumbled.

"Because it was the right thing to do."

Chapter Nine

"So, where are we?"

Draven's voice drifted out onto the balcony and Arin ran a hand through his hair. "No closer than we were a tick ago," he admitted.

"Where's Terra?"

"In the office," he replied, turning away to lean on the railing. Like his friend had in the days before, he wanted to rip the Rustac apart. Tear it to shreds in all reality, but he didn't. He somehow remained calm. Folding his arms, he sighed. "She is monitoring for a stone from Haydn."

Draven joined him. "I wish there was something that would make this easier."

He chuckled dryly. "There is not, but I do appreciate the sentiment."

His friend opened his mouth to say something else but was interrupted by Terra's voice. "Haydn just checked in."

They both whirled and he spoke before his oldest friend could. "And?"

Terra gulped, shifting from one foot to the other. He'd never, ever seen her nervous and it worried him. "She, she." There was a pause and he could see the indecision clear as daylight on her face and in the blue-silver swirls of her eyes. "They will head to Gahroon next," she finally whispered. "They plan, they are going to bomb it too."

He pushed off the railing and took her arms in a hard grip, almost shaking her but managing to hold it back at the last beat of his heart. "What!?"

Terra put a hand on his chest, stilling him and his anger as she gave the rest of it. "According to what she's been able to ply from the troops, they are reloading the bombs and will make a run at your home in two days."

He dropped his hands and staggered back, stopping only when he bumped into the railing. "They, they, would not. That, would kill..." He paused to do a quick calculation in his head and the potential was unbelievable. "Nearly half-a-million of, of my people."

Terra wrapped her arms around her stomach, her face falling.

Draven took the initiative and folded her against his chest. Tucking her under his chin, his brightly glowing eyes came to his. "We will not let that happen."

Terra pushed back enough to finish the report from his love. "She has help and plans on bringing down the three bombers before they ever reach the Buttes."

Hope flared to life in his chest and he pushed off the railing again. "Who? How?"

Terra laid her cheek against Draven's shoulder and let out a long sigh. "Four fairies managed to stow away on one of the ships. Between them..."

The implications hung there and the hope he'd just been feeling, died a cruel death. "She will be caught."

Draven growled low and long. "Not if we are there to help."

***

Two rotations later, Lunk the Fairy and his three siblings crawled over the engines, his younger sisters deep in the middle of an argument as they headed for

83

the spots Haydn had designated.

"I most certainly did not kiss him!" That denial was from Tafin, the oldest of the three.

"Oh you most certainly did!" Ellas, the middle of them, rebutted. "I saw you!"

"Ladies, ladies, let us not argue at this present time," Gali, the youngest, threw in. "It matters not who kissed who, does it?"

He rolled his eyes, leading them along the pipes of the compartment. Fortunately no one was on board presently, so he didn't worry about being discovered. Still, the fight they were having was ridiculously silly and had been going on for more than a few rotations.

Ellas stomped her small foot, the sound muffled by the large pipe. Well, large as compared to them at least. Just under a few inches tall each, they usually didn't even register to the naked eye. Which is why Haydn the Orc had asked them to partake in this particular mission, once she'd found them anyway.

"It does matter," Ellas whined. "Lalor was my intended, not yours Tafin."

He rolled his eyes again. Only *his* sisters would be fighting over a mate at a time like this. They were embarking on the most dangerous task any of them had ever faced and the triplets were more concerned over a man than the mission.

Women!

"That is enough," he finally interceded. "You can settle the matter when we return home."

As the oldest, and the family patriarch, that should have ended any and all discussion. But, his sisters had never, ever listened to him before and certainly didn't start now.

To Free The Dragon's Soul

"No!" Ellas stomped her foot again. "We will settle this now..." She drew her sword and poked her older sibling.

Tafin turned, drawing her own Fairy sized weapon, grinning widely. "Fine," she snorted, her blue wings fluttering in excitement. "To blood."

Oh by the Gods of all the Kingdoms!

He turned around, stepped between them and held out his hands. "Enough. This can wait."

Ellas' chest puffed out and she lifted off the pipe with her red wings going a length a heartbeat, zipping around him to attack the oldest triplet with a battle cry.

Gali, always the sensible of the trio, took him by the hand and pulled him out of the way. "Let them have it, brother. You know they will not cease their drither until they fight it out."

"Ugh! Why did the Gods curse me with you lot..."

He headed off again, listening to the pair's swords clashing as Gali fell into step with him.

She reached up and patted his arm consolingly. "At least they will not kill each other. It is only to blood."

He slapped a hand over his eyes, shaking his head. He couldn't argue with her either, that was the worst part. His sisters had always settled matters in this fashion, since they were first able to hold a sword. Still, now was not the time for such shenanigans. They had a mission, an important one, far more important than the sabotage they'd previously managed before the fleet had left Bra'ka.

Many lives were depending on the havoc the four of them were going to have to create before the ships reached Gahroon.

If they failed, or were distracted...

The ramifications of such a thing were too mind-numbing to contemplate. They mustn't fail. They couldn't. He wouldn't let them.

***

Haydn stood at the aft railing of the *N'Val*, watching the horizon behind them for any signs of Arin and the others. Her heart skipped over itself, hoping her message had gotten through. She'd had to send it quickly and didn't have time to wait for a response. She could only wait at this point.

If her plan got through, they would come, she was as sure of it as her next breath. If it didn't, well, she'd still do what she and the Fairies intended. She wasn't about to let Arin's people be destroyed...

"See anything?"

She turned toward the soldier. "Not a thing."

He slapped her on the back and she barely contained a growl. "Keep a careful eye. We do not want those crossbreeds to see us coming."

She dipped her chin and waited for him to walk away before breathing a soft sigh of relief.

So far, her infiltration had gone off without missing a beat. As she'd suspected, no one recognized her as The Shadow Flame, the nickname she'd often used in the Arena as Chieftain Zuor's assassin. Not for the first time, she was thankful she'd always worn the mask and hood during her fights. Her secretive life was paying off and in a good way.

In the distance a burst of red and orange lit the night, catching her attention.

The signal.

She waited six heartbeats and let out a shrill whistle to let Lunk and his siblings know it was time to begin. She had no idea what Arin would do, but she could flow with it, whatever it was.

She was nothing if not adaptive…

Which was probably going to get them both killed!

Arin dropped from the sky with a roar, landing on the ship with deck rattling shudder. He roared a second time and the momentary shock of his appearance wore off quickly as her fellow Orcs surrounded him.

With a wide grin, she pushed through the group. "Back off, I will take this."

The others laughed, cheering her on with a clatter of weapons.

She spun one of the short swords she'd confiscated around lithely, smirking toward her lover. "Come on you son of a Harpy, take your best shot."

Arin's right head beamed, his sharp teeth catching the lights around the vessel's railing. "With pleasure, Orc," he sneered.

And she almost believed him. If she hadn't known who he was, she might have a concern. But, she did know him and at the last possible thump of her heart, she dodged, spinning under his snapping jaws.

One of her brethren wasn't so lucky and met with a gruesome demise under her true love's assault.

Arin's left maw spit the Orc's head toward the others and turned her way again. "Hold still you miserable wench," the right growled.

She laughed, twirling away with a flourish. "I will not. Come and get me!"

Arin did just that, advancing with a menacing bellow. For a second time, she ducked under his snarling faces and her brother Orcs suffered for it. Her Mate reared up and came crashing down on two, using his razor sharp claws to split their chests open from neck to navel. His tail swished around and impaled a third, who screamed loudly as he was lifted and heaved away by the prehensile appendage. He whirled around and kicked out with a rear hoof, sending yet another after the one he'd dispatched with his tail.

Twice more they followed the same pattern, eradicating another ten of the troops before the ones remaining figured out all was not as it seemed.

The last seemed to wake up to their tactics just as Draven and Terra dropped from the dark clouds above and landed on the ship next to them with teeth vibrating shrieks.

"What the Nether…" one said too late.

The King and Queen laid into the crew and the vessel itself, smashing through the magically enhanced armor plating that kept it in the air. Bit by bit, as the coverings were clawed away, the craft began to angle toward the ground, spilling Orc and Ogre alike over the sides.

As the last piece was shredded, the boat relinquished its hold over gravity and plummeted toward the desert below. The few remaining crew's screams punctuated the darkfall, but there was nothing they would be able to do to save themselves.

The third craft exploded, spewing fire and smoke as it too nose-dived for the desolate land that stretched between the port and Gahroon. She searched the descending ship and finally spied the four colored specks lifting from the wreckage. Half a tick passed before the Fairies managed to fly back and land on the

88

railing.

She scooped the siblings onto her hand and held out a finger for the oldest to shake. "Well done."

Lunk wiped grime and soot off his cheeks and cracked a smile, taking her finger with his small hand. "It was a pleasure."

She grinned just as Draven and Terra shifted above the deck and landed on the bow.

"Where is that bastard?" Terra bellowed.

She stepped into her path, holding up a blood-covered hand. "Easy, My Queen. He remained in Rosau."

She snarled. "Then that is where we shall go."

Draven took that moment to intercede. "*Kyleri*, not yet. We will take the *N'Val* back to Win-ra. I want the Harpies to examine these bombs. Maybe they can come up with a counter to whatever poison is in them."

She nodded her concurrence, waving at the dead. "From what they were saying, these are not the only ones."

Lunk spoke up, lifting off her hand to hover in front of the human. "They are right. There is an entire warehouse of them in Bra'ka and they are making more."

That stopped Terra dead in her tracks and her anger visibly dissipated. "How, how many more?"

The Fairy sighed and tucked the wrench in his hand into his belt. "They are assembling several a rotation, Your Majesty. Within a couple they could easily fill another three ships..."

***

Terra stared across the way at the Harpies going about their business as if they didn't have a care in the world and for just a breath, she wanted to rage at all of them.

Didn't they know there was a war on? Didn't they realize the lengths evil was willing to go to, to win?

If they did, they didn't care apparently. Draven had said they'd remained oblivious to outsiders unless there was a profit to be made and had always reminded him of Goblins. He'd added in the next breath, they weren't the fighters they'd once been and preferred to heal nowadays.

"What is that phrase you use? A pen for your thoughts? Is that it?"

She smiled over her shoulder, exhaling softly. He'd been trying so hard over the last week or so to win her over again that she finally decided to cut him some slack. At least a little. "Something like that."

He came to the railing and reclined back against it. Facing the suite, he ignored the hubbub of the citizens. "So, what are you thinking, *Kyleri*?"

She propped her chin on her palm, tapping her fingers against her cheek. "That without Haydn, tonight would have had a far different outcome."

His lips pursed. "I agree."

The sun was just beginning to peek through the trees, throwing beams here and there to start a new day. It had taken them most of the night to pilot the *N'Val* back to the jungle domain and she knew it hovered somewhere off to the right and above them. A few of the Harpies had boarded at their request and were examining the bombs still loaded in her belly. What would or could come from it, she had no clue, but it was a start. It would be even better if they could do it again. In Bra'ka.

But, she was loath to ask Haydn to go undercover a second time.

As if reading her thoughts, Draven spoke in a calm, sure voice. "She is on her way."

She groaned and ran a hand through her hair. "And Arin? How did he take it?"

Her mate blew out a lungful of air. "He went with her."

She pinched the bridge of her nose. "Oy vey…"

He chuckled and laid a hand on her back. "I feel much the same. But, we are needed here. Haydn said this is not finished. The plan to bomb Gahroon was only the first stage. Carax and the remaining troops are already heading for the Butte's…"

Chapter Ten

Tian Dyran cradled the youngish looking Naiad against his chest. The cold river washed over and around them, sending a shiver through his entire body.

The woman snuggled closer, a soft sigh cracking out of her throat.

He dipped a shaking hand into the current and cupped some water into his palm. Carefully holding her with one arm, he allowed the substance to dribble into her mouth.

She struggled to swallow and he stroked her throat, helping just as he had for the last four rotations.

He shivered again, the frigid temperature sinking deep into his bones. The Kingdoms were just a few rotations away from the bitter cold season and it showed in the drastic difference of the water.

Since he'd sent her message to the Crone Mother, this had been their routine. She'd burn through the night, cursing and yelling herself hoarse in her delirium until his hearts just couldn't take it. At which point he'd carry her to the canal, allowing her to submerge until only her face showed and stay there.

There were no illusions that the stream had some sort of magical properties and would heal her, it hadn't so far, but it did have a soothing effect. And for that, he was grateful.

When *he* could no longer take the chill though, he'd have to return to their small camp and within a few ticks, the cycle would start all over again. And each time she bolted upright and began to curse him, his mother, his father, his brothers and sisters and anyone else that seemed to cross her deranged fever-state, his own hearts tore apart over his helplessness to fix this.

Now, he stroked her forehead with shriveled fingers and laid a tender kiss on her still scorching skin. Sweat beaded under his lips and he sighed. Other than to still her frenzied cries and rantings, his submersion technique had had little effect on the toxin induced sickness clutching her in its deadly grip.

"When did you last sleep, Tian?"

He scrubbed his eyes with numb fingers, cutting a look over his shoulder toward Dain and countered the question with a rhetorical sounding snort. "What rotation is it?"

Dain's left head sniffed indignantly. "That is what I thought." His right eyed the woman, its forehead dipping into a deep frown. "Why are you bothering?"

He turned back and drew her closer, staring across at the far bank and answered with a clatter to his teeth he could no longer hide. "I, honestly, do not, know."

Dain's massive right paw scratched at the dirt on the bank, directing him to exit the icy flow. "Come now, enough of this. You have done all you can."

He whipped around, barely holding back a growl. "*I* will say when it is enough, Dain."

The unusually colored, pure white Chimera was one of the few he'd ever considered a real friend. He had backed up a step at the vehemence in his voice, despite the clack of his teeth. "I—I meant no disrespect, Alpha," the left head said. "I, will go," the right added.

War Dog excrement was better than he was right then. "Dain," he amended, gentling his tone. "I am just tired."

Dain dropped a foreleg, bending both heads in

93

submission. "Yes, Alpha. I will leave you to it then."

His friend disappeared into the trees, heading back in the direction of their impromptu camp and he wanted to kick his own ass. He shouldn't have snapped. He rarely did, but Dain's attempts to sway him toward giving up brought it out of him.

He wouldn't give up, not like he had before, with his father.

Granted his father wasn't sick with a toxin, but he was mad and Tian had walked away from him. He'd left the former Alpha to fend for himself under the Buttes of Dashta. Abandoned the man who'd raised him without a backward glance.

By the time he'd changed his mind and returned, it was too late. His father was gone, lost to the grief induced dementia of losing his mate. Seeing the man's deranged state, he'd vowed then and there, to never allow another that close to his hearts.

Ever.

The woman moaned weakly and curled her face against his upper arm, the raging fire under her skin trying to burn him too, despite the wintry cold of the water.

Curling one hand around her cheek, he brushed a thumb just under her eye. "What have you done to me?" he whispered. "Why can I not walk away and leave you to your fate?"

A chuckle drew his gaze back up and he snarled. He tightened his hold, ready to shift and fly her away from any potential threat despite the chill in his bones. "Who is there?"

A blue haired head broke the surface, followed by the snout of a seahorse. "I am Mithrin." He slipped off the mount and swam the rest of the way with sure strokes, stopping when the water reached his waist. "And I do believe that is my sister you are holding."

***

"How is she?" he asked the moment Mithrin emerged from the tent.

The other Naiad ran a hand down his face and let out a long sigh. "The healing drink I brought will help, but she is far from well. What happened?"

He leaned against a nearby tree, only a bit of relief pulsing through his chest at the news. "I do not know," he said for the second time in as many ticks. "I found her not far from here. She had three Ogre arrows in her. I removed them and stitched her up as best I could. I did not know they were coated with a toxin." He paused and asked, "Did the Crone Mother send the medicine for her friend?"

Mithrin blinked slowly. "She did not send me. I came on my own after we intercepted your message."

His hearts punched together. "So, the message did not go through?"

The other man shrugged. "That I do not know. It may have." A sheepish look roamed through the sea-blue color of his eyes. "I did not wait after it was translated in all honesty."

He frowned. "Why? What is the rush?"

Mithrin turned enough to see the tent and something akin to pain flickered over his expression in the waning daylight. "Because I promised her friend I would rescue her." His gaze came back around, the blue of his eyes prominent now. "Did Phara say where Lanni was?"

Well, at least he finally knew her name.

"No, I fear she did not. She fell into the toxin's lunacy before she could give me any details." He jerked his chin to the north, toward Bra'ka. "The rest of my team has gone ahead to see if they can find where she emerged from the shield."

Mithrin threw up his hands and paced away, cursing in a myriad of languages, including a few fish sounding ones.

And he finally knew where Phara got her penchant for it...

He chuckled and shook his head, interrupting the tirade. "I am sorry to not be of more help, but I appreciate you coming."

Mithrin's shoulders slumped and he joined him at the tree, propping a foot against the bark. "No, no, it is not your fault. I was just too hopeful."

"That?"

"I would find my heart, again."

Now, he could definitely understand those sentiments. He cut a look at the canvas covering. Definitely understand. "Tell me about her," he whispered, not realizing he'd spoken the words aloud until they were past his lips.

Mithrin's hand dropped to his shoulder. "That my friend, is a very long, very involved telling."

He shrugged, unable to take his eyes off the tent. "We have time, yes?"

***

"She did not!"

A male's voice she recognized as Mithrin's laughed outright at the three words. "Oh, yes, she did. She walked right up to the King himself and kicked him square in the shin!"

Another male laughed, rather loudly and she growled, albeit weakly.

"How old was she?"

Mithrin laughed harder. "Four Suns!"

"What did your parental do?" another male she didn't recognize asked.

"Neptune was fit to be tied by Octa-tentacles let me tell you boys. He turned red as the new Sun and fumed for a good six rotations over it. He would not speak to her at all," Mithrin continued to chuckle. "But the moment she batted those eyes at him, he was done and forgave the slight."

Oh By the very Gods, he was telling someone about the time she'd gotten mad at King Elfane's daughter...and the poor man had suffered her impulsive wrath when he tried to break up the fight they were having.

The sad part was, she couldn't even remember what it was over. Not now, anyway, but she'd never, ever lived it down.

She flopped an arm over her eyes, her cheeks coloring with embarrassment that had nothing to do with her remaining fever.

She was going to kill Mithrin, she really was.

When she was strong enough, which she wasn't.

But, she was feeling better.

Wait! If Mith was here, had he brought the medicine for Lanni?

He must have!

Slowly working herself out from under a heavy fur, she staggered to her feet. Reaching for one of the trees holding up the canvas, she pushed it back and stumbled into the fresh air. Drawing in a deep lungful, she spied Mith, a humanoid looking albino Chimera and another of his kind, not in humanoid form but also an albino, seated around a low fire.

Four heads turned her way as the air touched her skin...*all* of her skin and she looked down, only to realize she was a naked as the day she'd emerged from her mother's body.

Borrowing one of her father's favored phrases, she sagged, still too weak to try and hide her naturalness from the two strangers. "Well, *kramcesgor!*"

Strong arms that were definitely *not* her brothers, scooped her up before she buckled and cradled her gently against a wide chest.

She caught his amused, white colored eyes and a small smile played across his lips.

"Hello," he whispered gently. "Feeling better?"

She licked her dry lips and cleared her throat. "I was."

Her cheeks burned with mortification. She hadn't blushed this much in 200 Suns!

Mithrin's chuckle said he'd seen it too.

Yet another thing she wouldn't live down anytime soon. Tilting her head enough to see around the thickly corded arm of the Chimera supporting her, she shot her older brother a look that promised him pain, and lots of it, in the very near future.

Her rescuers voice rumbled under her ear, doing some not-so-unpleasant things to the sensations rolling through her gut.

"Let us get you some clothing, yes?"

She shifted her eyes back to his, managing a raspy reply. "That, would be, appreciated."

***

A tick or so later, they were back at the fire, and she was snuggled on the Chimera's lap, nestled in a set of rippling arms she could absolutely appreciate. Clothing turned out to be a clean fur. After he'd tucked her up in it, he'd refused to let her walk under her own steam and promptly carried her back.

Now, seated on a log, she looked across the low flames toward her brother. "Did, you bring the medicine?" she managed softly.

Mithrin shook his head. "I did not see that part of the message. I apologize. I was," He paused and a look she'd never seen before danced over the planes of his face. "Anxious, to get here. Is she well?"

Ok, this was new. He'd never, ever expressed interest in a female, of any race. Prior to now he'd been so busy learning under their father to care.

Or so she thought. But, clearly something had happened between him and Lanni during their time on the West Beach. It was right there in his eyes.

And for the first time in her long life, she put aside sibling rivalry and spoke honestly, even though she hated herself for it and knew he probably would too, when she finished at least. "I do not know," she began. Her voice was feeble, scratchy and she detested that almost as much as the news she was having to impart. "She was barely functioning when I left."

Mith's throat worked and his reply came out nearly

as fragile as her own. "I never...I should have taken her, with me."

She wanted to console him, but he was out of easy reach. She inclined a look at her new protector and sluggishly pushed away from his natural heat. The smell of desert, dry yet clean drifted off him and she did her best to ignore the tingle it inspired in her abdomen.

With slow, weak steps, she shuffled around the pit and sank down next to her only sibling. Leaning against his side, she mumbled the best solace she could offer. "Lanni is strong, Mith."

He swiped at his cheeks and blew out a shaky breath. "I know. I just hope it is enough."

She wormed a hand free of the fur and gripped his forearm with as much strength as she could muster. "At first daylight, I will take you too her. How much Spring did you fetch?"

He smiled a bit. "Enough. If we are in time."

A heavy, disapproving snort drew her eye. Tian, as she'd come to find out, was scowling at them both.

"What?"

He rose to his impressive height, all seven feet of him. The dying embers flickered shadows across his features and something in her very core sprang to life. At first she thought it was left over from her fever, but this was a different sort of heat. It built quickly, spiraling outward to sizzle across every nerve, every hair and every pore of her body.

"What?" she rasped again.

He strode around the glowing coals and promptly, if all too tenderly, gathered her up. "You will go nowhere," he grunted. "You are too weak."

Chapter Eleven

"Has he confessed her location?"

"Nay Sire, he refuses to speak."

A grunt and a heavy sigh followed that statement and Rygan cracked a swollen eye toward the two in the corner of his cell.

"What have you tried?" Tyleios Cannis asked.

His torturer, a Hobgoblin, wiped blood covered hands on a small towel. "Short of plucking his wings feather by feather, everything."

The Satyr's shoulders stiffened and he snorted softly, growling out a command that sent true fear slithering down his spine. "Then do it."

He'd lost count of how long he'd been in this tiny little room, strapped to the table but it felt like a lifetime. Still, he would not give up Lanni's location no matter what they did. He couldn't.

"Your Majesty, there is no need to go that far."

He knew that voice and his heart hammered in his chest, breaking as it rushed the blood to his ears through the haze of pain. Turning, he spied Niar scramble up Tyleios' leg and perch on the rulers shoulder.

"I know where the human is."

He arched against the hard steel on his wrists, invigorated by the Ferret's betrayal. "No! Niar! You cannot!"

A sly grin parted the small creatures face and he could see the glow of treason in his eyes, even from here. He turned back to Cannis, the smile never faltering. "Come Your Highness, I will take you right to her."

Rygan bellowed in anguish, thrashing against the metal holding him prisoner. It did no good and he could only watch helplessly as the son of Furiem and the wrongful ruler of Bra'ka left without a backward glance.

"Sire? What should I do with the prisoner?"

Cannis paused in the doorway. "Continue. We must know all it does before we kill it."

***

"You must go!"

Rinsa turned at the urgency in the voice. "I am sorry?"

Kulth, one of the Halfling Council of the Undermarket, rushed into the room and his short, stubby fingers began unplugging the machines. "You *must* go," he said again. "They are already at the other end of the Market!"

"We, we cannot," he managed. Jerking into action, he moved between the balding humanoid and Lanni's life support. "She will not survive."

Kulth drew up and jerked a small finger over his shoulder. "It is better she die trying to live than be taken and killed yes?"

A hard, shocked sounding gasp drifted across the room and Rinsa turned from the impasse with the Halfling. A handsome Naiad with long blue hair filled the opening but he didn't stay there long.

"Lanni," he whispered, striding forward much as Kulth had done moments before. He bent over the bed, gathering the human into his arms. Cradling her against his shoulder, he kissed her face, muttering something unintelligible. He pulled back and lifted a small flask from his waist.

Rinsa had been in the healing arts for many Suns but he didn't recognize the greenish hue to the water the man allowed to dribble around the breathing tube he'd had to install shortly after Turosh had gone for the medicines he desperately needed. Rigged from whatever he could find, it'd been pushing air in and out of her lungs ever since. But now, several tense heartbeats after the fluid hit her system, whatever it contained seemed to counter the sickness that had plagued the poor girl. It didn't instantly heal her, but it was enough that she began to cough and choke around the tubing.

Her hands weakly curled into the dirty bedding and she arched against the Naiad's hold, sputtering slightly in response.

"Set her down," he commanded. The man laid her back again but kept hold of one of her hands as Rinsa worked. Bending close, he whispered gently, not knowing if she could or would hear and follow his instructions. "Exhale, if you can."

She, unbelievably, pushed out enough air and when it was cleared, she coughed again, harder and her eyes fluttered open. They blinked several times then focused, if briefly on her savior. "Mi—Mith?" she choked out.

He nodded, pushing Rinsa aside and gently ran his hands over her face, his voice crackling with emotions. "I am here love."

"You *must* go," Kulth insisted again.

The Naiad's eyes came up to his as Lanni's slipped closed again and she let out a long sigh. "Can I take her?"

He checked her vitals quickly, pleased to see the pulse in her neck gain an extra beat or two. He didn't like the idea of it, but what choice did they really have. From the panic in Kulth's tone, whatever or whoever was coming would either kill the woman instantly, or – from the tale he'd gotten out of Phara and the half-breed when they'd arrived – far worse. "Yes, go. I have done what I can."

The Naiad scooped her up, bedding and all and turned left out of the door, the way the other one had gone. Considering they were of the same race, Phara must have sent him. At least he hoped so and further hoped the human survived the trip.

***

Mithrin had never been so scared in his long life as he was making his way through the Undermarket and back to the sewer pipe. He'd come alone and thankfully his timing couldn't have been better.

Behind him, as he ducked into the access way leading to the pipe, he could hear the Ogre's, Orc's and Centaurs rampaging through the underground caverns. The Halflings that lived here and had sheltered his love, screamed angrily, but none of the ones who saw him seemed inclined to direct the forces his way.

And for that he would be eternally grateful.

When he reached the nasty smelling opening, he did the only thing he could and heaved Lanni's slight frame over his shoulder. "Forgive me, love," he whispered. "This is the only way."

She said nothing and he was relieved she'd passed

out again.

He would have gotten an earful otherwise.

Chuckling to himself, he worked his way through the muck and mire, just as Phara had done however long ago...

***

Phara paced, as least as much as Tian would allow, waiting, watching the end of the same pipe she'd spilled out of rotations before, for her brother. Tian's fellow Chimera's were not far away and she could feel their eyes on her from behind the trees.

The man himself though, stood silent sentry at the water's edge. His feet were braced, his hands folded into the small of his back and he grunted disapprovingly with every step she took.

"You will get sick again."

She harrumphed, already feeling stronger than she had the day before. He wasn't hearing it though. So, she didn't bother to rebut the statement.

Instead, she eyed the shadowed opening, willing it to spit out her sibling, as crazy as that sounded.

Had he found Lanni?

She tilted a look at the pulsing green shield over the city. It didn't seem any stronger or weaker to her eye, but she was no purveyor of magic. Still the energy stream pulsing off the King's Tower appeared steady, like it had when Garax...

She cut that off. She would mourn her unlikely friend another time. When this was all said and done, she'd give the Ogre the service of gratitude he deserved for his sacrifice.

105

A coughing, retching sound echoed out into the darkfall and relief wormed its way along her nerves. Several tense heartbeats followed and Mith, covered from head to toe in muck and grime, emerged. He had one arm wrapped around something on his shoulder and he bent long enough to expel the small meal they'd consumed just before leaving their camp at the crack of daylight.

She checked the hill above, watching the same direction the Ogre's who attacked her had appeared from.

Nothing.

Good.

Mith stumbled a step, his grunge covered boots slipping in the grass as he carefully, tenderly slid the bundle off his shoulder.

She recognized Lanni's fire-red hair and another wave of relief pumped through her veins. She moved then, galvanized by their escape. "How is she?" she asked, meeting him halfway from the lake.

Mithrin coughed again and shifted the bundle in his arms. He continued walking and she fell into step, holding a finger under Lanni's nose. Air pushed out of her lungs and drew back in, but it was very weak.

"Alive," her brother managed as Tian met them.

Her Chimera protector let out a long whistle and the flap of wings overhead drew her gaze up. His team of five landed near the water and Dain turned to the side, ready to take them away.

An arrow sang through the air and thunked into the meaty part of albino's flank. He reared up with a loud roar and she pulled the bolt out, tossing it to the ground with a sneer. Hopefully she was in time, before too much of the toxin entered his system.

"Go, go, go," she yelled at her brother.

Drawing her sword, she turned to face whatever enemy had either happened upon the group or followed him from the Undermarket.

Sadly, it was both.

Orcs poured out onto the grassy incline and more arrows thumped into the ground at their feet from atop the hill.

"Go!" she urged again, bumping her hip into Mithrin's. "We will hold them off."

Tian wasn't about to let that happen though. He growled and wrapped his hands about her waist at the same time Mithrin was securing Lanni across Dain's back. He lifted her on to his fellow Chimera and gave his second a slap across the withers. "Now!"

Without hesitation, the creature lifted into the air. She twisted back, fuming that he'd be so high-handed and her last sight as they cleared the nearby trees, was of her brother and her Chimera squaring off to face the coming onslaught of Ogre's, Orc's and Centaurs…

***

Tian waited just long enough to see Dain get out of range before he shifted and met the enemy head on with a ground shaking roar.

"Well, this is fine mess," Mithrin grumbled, taking out the first to reach them with a flashing swipe of his blade.

His right head grunted while his left sank his long teeth into the throat of the nearest, green-skinned assailant. "Indeed."

107

Ripping through the creature's neck, it fell away, blood spurting across the fur on his face. Unfortunately, he was only to be replaced by another. He growled, slashing through one after another after another.

An arrow creased his shoulder and he hissed, eyeing the troops on the hill.

"Rydor, Targ, take them out."

The two in question, lifted off the ground, respectfully shaking several as they spun high and subsequently dive bombed the four Ogre's and two Centaurs vantage point. Another arrow stung across his back and he growled, taking the pain out on the nearest Orc he could get to.

Mithrin was holding his own. He spun through the moonlight, his weapon flashing and singing against the cold air, felling three in rapid succession. Two more circled him, but the Naiad had clearly seen his share of battle and he had them well in hand.

Another of their kind emerged from the pipe and he could see she was, well different. A blue face momentarily smiled at him as she paused in the opening then was covered by her own hand as she slipped a black mask into place. Pulling up a thick hood, he lost sight of her as she melded with the shadows. He caught her again, well, more like the red-orange glow of the fire-coated blade in her hand before it sunk deep into the back of one of her own kin.

Whoever she was, she was on their side apparently and he let her have at it.

They could use all the help they could get!

She felled two and paused, catching his eye across the moonlit battle field.

He jerked a nod toward the scene above. Targ had

been pulled to the ground by two of the massive brutes, who now held him by the wings as a Centaur took aim with one of the toxin laced arrows.

She didn't hesitate and lithely ran up the embankment. Launching into the air, he was impressed as she landed across the horse's half of the Centaur and ran him through from behind.

Targ bent a wing, yanking one of the Ogre's off balance and flung him toward the newest addition to their side with a wicked looking grin spreading across his right face. The Orc stood up on the Centaurs back and again, launched herself into the air, slamming blade first into the stumbling enemy...

He turned back to his own issues and not a heartbeat too soon. Several of the beasts were approaching, swords up and ready and he met them willingly. He split the first's chest wide with a side swipe of his powerful claws and let the momentum carry his swing into the second. His long talons stuck in the leathery flesh and the distraction of shaking it free was his undoing.

"Tian!"

A third, smaller of the minions had managed to sneak up on him from behind. Letting out a pain filled bellow, he spun, his right head biting the Orc nearly in half in response. But the damage had been done and he caught the gleam of the hilt buried deep in his wither's a hearts beat before he collapsed onto his side...

Chapter Twelve

"What do you mean she escaped?"

"I am sorry, Master, but the human managed to get away."

"How?"

There was an audible gulp and Fallon was half-tempted to turn around and see who the Unicorn was arguing with. Half-tempted. But she didn't. Instead she kept her eyes firmly pinned on the screens in front of her. It didn't stop her from listening though...

"As near as I can see, Master," a voice nervously echoed from one of the monitor's at Malice's station. "She was taken from the Undermarket."

Golix's question came out on more of a growl and she actually pitied the poor sap he was addressing. "By whom?"

Another audible gulp. "A Naiad."

The Unicorn's hoof cracked against the wood floor. "What!?"

He was apparently not expecting that answer and it didn't make a lick of sense to her anyway. She continued to listen though. The more info she had, the better her chances of getting Grams, Gramps and Fyris out of this.

"How could you let this happen Cannis!?" His hooves clacked as he paced away from Malice's bank of computers and then back again. "They never get involved."

She cut a look over her shoulder, almost gasping aloud at the image taking up several of the screens. She had no idea what to call the creature but he had a goat's head and long horns that reminded her of a ram, curled over and back behind his long twitching ears.

His eyes darted around nervously and he gulped again, his short neck all but hiding his Adams apple. "I am sorry, Master," he stammered. "I had no idea they were involved either..."

The apology was weak at best and she had the feeling if the poor guy was in the room, he'd be dead for it.

Smoke coiled out of Golix's nostrils in a huff. "What happened after she was taken? Why did your troops not stop them?"

The goat-man thing on the screen nodded to someone out of camera range and the display changed. His image was replaced with a scene right out of some sort of Fairy Tale. Orcs ran down a grassy hill, attacking four of the strangest two-headed lions she'd ever seen. Ogre's fired arrows down at the group, while two Centaurs straight out of mythology galloped back and forth behind them. There was no audio to it, but she didn't need it as the battle played out.

The dual-headed lion things seemed to be winning but then the tide turned when one was stabbed viciously and fell over. The others gathered him up and retreated quickly out of frame, lifting off the ground with beats of their powerful looking wings.

At first she could only blink at it, thinking it looked like something out of that old vid, *Lord of the Rings*, but from the furious bellow that came from Golix, she got the distinct impression it had actually happened and not too long ago either.

"I do not care what you have to do," the black beast growled viciously when the battle scene ended.

111

"Find the human and find her now!"

"Yes…"

The rest was cut off by Malice. Her fellow hacker shot a worried look up at Golix. "Sorry Boss. Anything I can do?"

She turned away, dropping her head quickly. Her savings grace over the last four days was she'd remained quiet and demure, even though it grated on everything she was. He had the leverage though and they both knew it.

Tapping away at the keys, she ignored the rest of their conversation, trying to make sense of what she'd just seen. Sad part was, she couldn't. There was no such thing as two-headed lions, or goat-men or Ogre's or Orcs or Centaurs, except in the Fairy Tales her cousin Terra adored.

Right?

Right!

Then again, there was no such thing as Unicorns either but here she was being held prisoner by one and her long-time rival was in league with him too!

None of this made sense. At all.

So, what did?

Had she fallen asleep with her vid-helm on again?

No. No. She clearly remembered the fight with Byron that started it all. He'd come home, yelled at her for something asinine, hit her and stormed out again. And it was the last straw. Almost a solid year of his mocking, verbal abuse and getting punched in the gut was the breaking point.

Not a minute after he left, she hacked into Uni-Air, booked a 'paid-for' flight and was out the door with a few creds in her pocket and the clothes on her back.

She should have cleaned the bastard out, she could have and hidden in the farthest destination she could find.

But no, she'd run home, to Scotland and met one sexy-as-hell Dragon. Well, according to Gramps he was a Dragon and from what she'd seen of his behavior since he'd been captured, she was starting to believe it.

Discretely, she punched a few keys in the midst of her typing and pulled up a small window in the corner of her screen. The tiny display showed the same three rooms that were on one of Malice's monitors a few feet away.

Grams sat in the middle of hers, legs crossed and hands folded primly in her lap. The only thing missing was the knitting she usually had close at hand. If she had been doing that, Fallon would have thought they were back in their living room...

Gramps slowly paced his, hands folded to the small of his back. From the scowl furrowing his forehead, he was plotting something but what she didn't know...

Fyris was her real concern. Even four days later, he still raged at the captivity. He alternated between pounding on the walls, clawing at them and slamming his shoulder into the reinforced cinder blocks...

None of which had done him a bit of good, then or now. Her heart broke at the sight of his bloody knuckles, torn clothing and disheveled, almost panicked appearance. She had no idea why he was acting this way, what the root cause might be, but something had set him off, in all the wrong ways.

She closed the window again, unable to take it, though she couldn't explain that reaction, even if she tried.

"You about done there bitch?"

She swiped at the tears in her eyes and cleared her throat, giving into the snarkiness she'd been holding in. "You know, if this was easy, you could do it you slack-jawed, greasy-haired twat!"

She screeched when Malice wrapped his long fingers into her hair and yanked her head back. His putrid breath fanned over her face.

"I hope the Boss man lets me kill you when he's done with ya."

She pulled away and spun her chair. Bringing up a foot between his legs, she nailed him right in the cajones and grinned when he doubled over with a girly sounding yelp. Grabbing his chin, she pinched it hard. "Just try it."

"Enough!"

She pushed Malice away again and looked up at Golix. "What? He started it."

The bastard's one red eye rolled and he snorted out something that sounded like, 'children' before leaving the office.

"You'll, pay, for, that," Malice gasped. Still clutching a hand between his legs, he staggered to his feet and followed the Unicorn.

The door swished closed behind them, leaving her alone. She harrumphed and turned back to her station. She knew better than to use Malice's. She'd already tried, the first time they'd left her alone. When they'd returned the next morning and found her 'tracks' in his system, Golix had knocked her out of the chair and kicked her several times.

She touched her still tender ribs and sighed softly. She'd not made that mistake again. Instead, she back doored into Malice's network and while she didn't have full control of it, she could still use it to her advantage.

Pulling up the screen with her family and Fyris on it, she pressed the button to connect to the intercom in their respect rooms, keeping her voice barely above a whisper. "Can you guys hear me?"

Grams opened her eyes but didn't move. Gramps stopped and tilted his head. Fyris, however did not respond. He continued to pace and punch, pace and punch and the anxiety that fairly rolled off him in a wave, even on camera, scared her.

Grams was the first to speak. "Fallon? Are you hurt?"

"No, I'm fine." she hissed. "Now, listen closely..."

***

It was the worst plan. Ever. His granddaughter couldn't be serious about this. There was no way he could follow through with it, nor would it work.

"Yes, it can and we will Thorak."

He snorted at the voice that had lived in his head for a 1,000 years. And replied. *"Yes, dear."*

Decia, the love of his life, *his Kyleri*, snorted back. *"You don't trust your own granddaughter?"*

"Oh, I trust her, *just not that bastard of a Unicorn. For all we know, he could be watching her and already know her intent."*

Decia's, or Diana now, disdainful sniff echoed across the connection that had formed when they mated an eon ago. The same link that had plagued him, haunted him, and scared him, more than a time or two.

"I heard that."

He sighed. "*I know you did. You always do. But, about this plan of* your *grandchild's...*"

"*Oh, now she's* my *grandchild...*"

He knew the rant that was coming and tuned her out, at least for a moment, but as she always did, she caught him not listening. A burst of displeasure smacked him mentally between the eyes and he sighed again. "*Very well. We will do it her way. But, I still do not like it.*"

***

Golix paced his inner sanctum, working out this latest development and how he could counter it. He'd always counted on getting the human back and returning her to the energy stream to finish the spell. Once she died within it, the shield over Bra'ka would remain for all time, leaving the only entrance and exits points under his direct control.

With her escape, however, everything changed.

He either needed to send a contingent of troops after her, again, or find another of...

He stopped dead.

Could it truly be that simple?

Of course it could. And the utter brilliance of the idea was enough to send happy shivers over his flanks.

Returning to the room where he'd set up the computers, he found Malice asleep at the wide, U-shaped desk.

Fallon had been taken to her room, just off this one and he checked the monitor to find her curled up in the corner, sound asleep and oblivious to the new part she would play.

116

The human hacker jolted awake when he kicked the back of his chair. "I'm up, I'm up." He blinked, rubbed his eyes and yawned. "What's up Boss Man?"

"Has she finished what we need?" he asked without preamble.

Malice yawned a second time, wiped more grit out of his eyes with a knuckle and nodded. "Sure. Enough of it. I can do the rest." A slow smile spread over his rodent like features. "Can I kill her now?"

"No. Connect me with Cannis."

Malice's face fell but he turned to the keyboards and did as he was bade. The moment the Satyr's face filled the screen, he rattled off his new orders. "Gather the Herd. I need another portal."

Tyleios yawned too and he snorted in disbelief. Why was it so hard to find reliable minions!

"Did you hear me Cannis?"

The Satyr nodded slowly. "Yes, Master. When would you…"

He cut the beast off. "Now!"

***

Right on cue, at the exact stroke of midnight, the lock on his cell, hissed, twisted and the door creaked open by a hair's breadth. Tom scrubbed a hand over his face, let out a sigh and eased it back the rest of the way.

As Fallon had said, the hallway beyond was empty. She'd managed to rotate the Guard's shift change to midnight, instead of 11 p.m., which gave her the perfect opportunity to open their cells for them to escape.

Without her.

Fyris, if he knew anything about Dragons, was not

going to like it. But maybe, from what he'd heard echoing out of the cell next to his, he wouldn't be cognizant of it either. At least he hoped not.

If all else failed though, he could always deck the poor lad and knock him out. Again.

The cells on either side of his had opened as well and Fyris burst into the hallway, bent over and drew the air into his lungs as if he had been starving for it this entire time.

Decia emerged from hers, much more calmly and joined him. Intertwining their fingers, she eyed her kin skeptically. "Is he well?"

"Fyris? Lad? Are you with us?"

The poor man remained bent over, hands on his knees and oh, so slowly nodded. "Where, is, she?" he managed around heaves at the stale, recycled air.

He exchanged a look with his wife. "In the penthouse."

Before either of them could say more, he was gone, tearing down the hall toward the door marked 'stairs'. He barreled through it and they easily heard his feet begin the long journey up 70 flights.

His wife's words were full of sympathy. "We should probably stop him."

He agreed and headed for the elevator. The doors opened on the first press of the button, Fallon having sent the car ahead of time for just this reason. The plan was for them to escape so Golix no longer had leverage. From there, she could sabotage his plans from the inside with her skills.

Sadly, it did not seem Fyris was going along with this plan.

He pushed the button for the 20th floor and the car

shot up rapidly. When they arrived, he calmly strode out, found the stairwell Fyris had taken, propped open the door...and waited.

Within a beat or two, the Dragon pounded into view, barely winded.

"There is a faster way lad."

He snorted and tried to push past, but Tom blocked him, pointing back to the car Decia was holding open.

"Fine," Fyris growled. Head bent, he spun and entered the elevator, tapping his fingers against his crossed arms the entire ride.

He couldn't blame the poor man, he knew all too well what it was to be separated from your mate for too long...

No one spoke on the way up, but in hindsight, he wished they had. It might have made what happened next, a tad easier to swallow.

He'd always heard about those moments when time stands still but had never experienced one until now. The elevator dinged, the doors opened again and his eyes took in an unbelievable scene.

Golix stood in the middle of the room. A small male, with stringy, greasy looking hair stood next to him. On the Unicorn's other side was a brute of a man, easily seven feet tall and looked like he could drop-kick a small car. Fallon struggled against the guy's firm grip on her arms, kicking and screaming more than a few obscenities he'd didn't even know she knew.

Just in front of Golix and this weird crew, a puddle had begun to waver and shimmy, undulating like ripples on a still pond. Magic crackled at the air, snapping and the hairs on the back of his neck stood on end. A loud

119

snap then a portal spiraled into existence.

On the other side, a semi-circle of five black Unicorns waited, their horns glowing brightly and before anyone could say anything, the brute pushed Fallon ahead...and they disappeared.

Chapter Thirteen

Tom Heegan had seen plenty of angry men in his long life...and the God's knew Diana's temper was nothing to sneeze at.

What he wasn't prepared for, was a Dragon in a full-out blood rage.

He'd never seen it, but, that's exactly what he got from Fyris.

The portal had no sooner closed with a thunderous crack than his anguished bellow reverberated across the foyer in which the Unicorn and other human remained.

Golix, for all his evil, actually turned a shocked expression their direction.

And it did his heart good to see he clearly hadn't known they were coming.

Fallon's plan, such as it was, would have worked. If they'd left as she intended, at least.

Again, time suspended itself for several beats then started up in fast-forward...and several things happened at once.

Fyris bent in half and like a defensive tackle of old, rushed out of the elevator toward the stunned beast and his human minion.

The human's eyes went wide and he spun on a heel, a feminine sounding shriek echoing in the wake of the Dragon's distressed howl. He tripped over his own feet, heading for a set of large double doors on the other side of the room.

Golix wasn't so easily moved and looked like he'd meet Fyris' charge head-on. He braced his hooves, pulled his head up and...laughed.

The noise sent shivers down his spine and jerked him into action. Reaching for Diana's kin, he tried to pull the man back but his grasping fingers met with empty air. The Dragon was intent on his target and not to be swayed from his goal.

The doors the human was heading for opened, spilling out twenty or so of the same men they'd faced when they first arrived. As a unit, they tackled Fyris before he got halfway across the room.

He held his own for a moment, throwing off the first few in his rage, but they bore him to the floor through sheer weight of numbers.

Which surprised him. They were armed to the teeth, everything from swords to automatic weapons hung from the thick vests they wore, but they didn't fire a single shot.

For now.

"I'll get him. Be ready love," Diana sighed softly.

"As always," he said, moving to hold the doors open with his body.

His wife, calm as you please, strode toward the struggling group of humans and the roaring, raging Fyris. Without pause, she kicked out, catching the poor lad in the chin and knocked him out cold.

Silence fell, save for her softly tapping foot and she crossed her arms. "Now that that nonsense is done, shall we negotiate?"

***

Fyris groaned, slowly returning to the land of the living. His brain throbbed, matching the staccato beat of his triple hearts. Blood rushed through every vein, ringing in his ears as he blinked open his eyes. He winced at the brightness and closed them again with another groan.

"Welcome back."

Diana's gentle voice drew his head around and he cracked an eye. "What, what happened?"

She pressed a cool cloth to his forehead and her fuzzy outline smiled. "You panicked."

He sniffed indignantly, turned his face away and flopped an arm over his eyes. "I most certainly did not."

But, he had. From the very instant he'd awakened in that, room, that's exactly what he'd done. At first, he thought he could control the building hysteria, but he'd lost that battle within the first ticks. Memories of another time, another room precisely like the empty, impersonal one he'd found himself in this time, had slammed to the forefront of his thoughts...

He shuddered and Diana's voice kept him from going there, again.

"You're safe now, Fyris. Rest easy."

He gulped and his response came out raspy and broken. "What, happened?"

Tom's deep baritone pounded through his aching head and jaw. "My wife saved your arse."

He shifted his arm, spying the Scot perched on the end of the couch near his feet. "What?"

He didn't bother to repeat himself, merely tilted his head toward the woman in question. He turned and dread replaced the aches and pains in his battered body with her explanation. The sad part was, the suffering was his own fault...this time.

"Golix no longer had need of us," she said quietly. "He let us go."

A brief flicker of recollection pushed through the haze thumping at his grey matter and his chest tightened. "Fallon," he whispered. "Did, he…" He couldn't get the words out, but Diana's pitying look and slow nod confirmed what wouldn't pass his lips. A shiver of fear coursed from his hair to his toes. "Why?"

Diana's shoulder lifted with a shrug. "I have no clue. But it won't be good."

He sat up, the hammering in his skull intensifying. "I, I have to go after her."

Diana pushed him back to the couch again. "In due time."

He flicked off her hand, rolling to his feet. Dizziness consumed him and he faltered. Tom was there and eased him back to the cushions.

"Easy lad. Easy."

He harrumphed at his own weakness and leaned his head back. Gathering his wits, he asked again, "What happened?"

Diana shifted up onto the seat and patted his thigh. "My granddaughter managed to override the locks on the cells. We were supposed to leave the building and negate the bastard's leverage."

He turned toward her. "I, I…"

She patted his thigh again, consoling him. "Understandably, you couldn't. The Mate Bond for us is stronger than with most."

"Us?"

Diana pulled a leg up and faced him directly. "Fyris, Dragon's from the Royal Lines have more advantages and the disadvantages to counter them." Her eyes roamed over him critically and he felt like a youngling about to be reprimanded. "Why don't we start with what caused your panic attack?"

He'd never told anyone about *that* time. Since his escape, he'd never mentioned it again, to anyone, even himself. "I was Golix's prisoner, before," he finally managed to say.

She tilted her head, brow furrowing slowly. "When?"

He drew in a lungful of air and shakily let it back out again. His thoughts drifted back, heightening the pulsating ache in his head and hearts. "Just before the last Great Wars ended," he began, tugging at a rip in his pant leg. "I was captured and sent to Ne'lo."

Diana gasped, one hand covering her mouth.

Today, the prison facility was the worst place to be sent. Situated dead center in the barren, icy wasteland of Mit'ctho, the 1st Kingdom, it was home to those citizens, of all races, that were beyond rehabilitation.

But back then, during the Wars, it had been home to The Herd. The Unicorns had used it as their base of operations during the conflicts. Carved out of a glacier of pure ice, it's blindingly white walls had driven more than a few prisoners completely insane.

And he'd almost been among them...

"Golix and his kind," he paused, his voice breaking on the next word. "Tortured, me. For fun. For information. Even to alleviate their boredom..."

Diana's hand dropped from her lips to his forearm, squeezing gently. "How long?"

Closing his eyes tightly, he ignored the single tear that escaped to slide down his cheek. "100 Suns..."

***

Dear Gods above, no wonder the poor man had nearly gone berserk in that cell. Diana could only imagine what had been going through his head when he woke up.

And it pissed her off. Royally pissed her off.

Pushing off the small couch of the private plane, she headed for the cockpit and poked her head around the door. "Change course."

One of the pilot's turned, quirking an eyebrow. "I'm sorry Ma'am?"

She growled, low and long. "Head for Casper. Wyoming."

The pilot's eyes widened and she knew her own were glowing the typical bright red of her kind.

His response quivered but he pressed the necessary buttons on the console at the same time. "Yes, Ma'am."

The jet tilted, banked over and headed back toward the U.S...

This had gone far enough. She'd been away from the Kingdoms for too long. In her absence, things had gone to hell in a hand basket and it was high time to rectify that.

"My love? Where are we going?" Tom asked carefully when she stormed by him toward the back of the plane.

"Home."

***

It had been an age and a half since Diana had thought of home, but the moment they crossed the barrier, all her old magics erupted through every pore of her body.

Dragons did age, albeit slowly, but as the power inherent to her kind coursed along her nerves and pounded through her blood, she felt, well, young again. She drew the air deep into her lungs and while a bit stale, it was still fresh and new and full of all the scents she remembered from her youth.

The newly bloomed Cayni trees that surrounded the mountain on this side…

The sickeningly sweet smell of the dying Sila grass just outside the cave's entrance as the cold began to settle across the 3rd Kingdom…

The fresh, clean, invigorating aroma of the cave's natural springs hidden deep under the cavern Enon had called home long before she was even a twinkle in her mother's eye…

"Decia?"

She laughed at the surprised tone in her fellow Dragon's voice and squatted on the ledge. "Hello old friend. How are you?"

His majestic head lifted into the air and without thought, she jumped, landing lithely on his snout. She could have just as easily shifted herself, but the space was too small for two Dragon's, must less three.

Tom and Fyris joined her a heartbeat later and her old mentor lowered them to the ground. They climbed off and he answered her question as they exited into the early evening a few moments later.

"I am well," he said. His head lowered again, one eye pinning her. "I was pleased to meet your offspring."

She laughed and patted the scales on his nose. "Thank you. What news do you have?"

He snuffled and a long burst of heated air washed

over them. "Not much, I fear. I am not in the know this far north."

She smiled softly. "But your work here is appreciated. Keep the portal safe."

"I always do."

With that, she walked away several feet and for the first time in a 1,000 years shifted into her true form. Her spine elongated, filling in with the age old memory of what she truly was easily enough. Long, leathery wings sprouted from her shoulders, expanding with a creaking snap of bone and flesh. Her legs and arms shaped into talon-laden paws with a crunching thwack and she dug them deep into the soil, reveling in the feel of the earth between her toes. Her teeth reformed into hard points and she yawned widely, stretching little used muscles.

A low whistle rang across the early evening. "I had forgotten how beautiful you were, *Kyleri.*"

She held out a newly formed paw and her husband climbed into it. Curling her talons around him, she chuckled. "And I'd forgotten how good this feels..."

Fyris shifted beside her and she eyed his only slightly smaller Dragon form. He was still young, comparatively speaking, but, he'd grow into it. His scales fluctuated from red to orange and back again then settled between the two. "I must go to Bra'ka."

She rolled her eyes. "From the sounds of things, that will do you no good, yes?"

He turned a red-orange orb her way. "I do not care."

He started to lift off and she wrapped her tail around his foot, dragging him back to the ground. "Do *not* make me hurt you, again."

He struggled against her hold, briefly, then seemed to see the reason in her words. When he stilled, she said, "Are the Cyclops still allies?"

Fyris slowly nodded. "Most of them. A few defected from what I heard."

She let go and flapped her own wings. "Then we shall head to Kyles. From there, we can contact Draven and figure out exactly what needs to be done."

***

Fallon couldn't believe her eyes. She just couldn't. But the evidence was right there. At first she'd been too busy fighting meat-heads grip to recognize the magic in the portal, but as it washed around her in the cross over, there was no denying what her eyes were seeing.

Surrounding them was another group of Unicorns like Golix. The brightness in their horns diminished quickly as they arrived but she turned back and had enough time to see the elevator open to reveal Grams, Gramps and Fyris.

Just before the portal closed, his anguished howl pierced the barrier and her heart twisted over on itself in equaling agony.

She'd never been one to believe in magic. Give her ones and zeros any day of the week and she was happy. Ecstatic even, but now, facing five Unicorns and several dozen of the goat-men, she had to question everything.

Just had to.

She looked to the nearest horned beastie and paused in her struggles with meat-head. "Ok, now, just what the hell is going on?"

Chapter Fourteen

One of the five Unicorns turned to the others, an indignant sniff huffing out of his snout. "Are all humans this insolent?" His four companions shrugged but said nothing. The one that had spoken nodded toward a door on the far side of the roof. "Take her below."

As meat-head pushed her along again, she got a look at the surrounding buildings and was amazed. They were as modern as Denver, stretching tall and proud toward the darkening sky. Lights were flickering on in the twilight and one window was close enough for her to see its occupant as he, or she, walked past.

It was really hard to tell much about the, thing, other than its coloring. Bright green and yellow feathers covered what she could see of it, shifting and catching the light in the room. Its matching yellow beaked face turned and pitch black eyes locked with hers. Its brows pinched down and something akin to pity flashed through its features before the moment was broken as it turned away again.

As they rounded the corner, she got another shock. Lining the wall next to the stairwell exit and the heating/cooling units was a group of more strange creatures. Some she recognized from the tales Gramps had told in her youth but most she didn't. There had to be twenty or so seated on the roof's gravel surface, all of them with their heads hanging.

"Come on you and you, up," one of the goat-men said.

She watched, partly fascinated but mostly horrified as two of the creatures, a goblin and a semi-humanoid, were dragged to their feet and shuffled forward with a prodding sword.

Falling to his knees, the humanoid begged. "No, no, please. I do not want to die…"

She had no idea what he was talking about, but the goat thing jerked him back to his feet and shoved him again. The poor man stumbled and fell, sliding toward a massive metal plate and the beam of energy pulsating from it. He managed to scream once before something caught a hold of him and yanked him into the bright white light stretching upward.

She tilted her gaze to follow its path and got yet another shock. High above, a curving, undulating wave of green stretched down toward the ground. Following it before meat-head could push her through the door, she shuddered, realizing it overlapped the entire city.

A terrified wail punctuated the night and drew her gaze back to the roof. Silent tears pooled in her eyes as the humanoid creature in the beam twisted and writhed, folding in on himself with a crunch and tear of bone and muscles…

And evaporated right before her eyes.

***

Mithin paced outside the trauma unit of the Cyclops medical facility. They'd been working on Tian for the last six ticks and he eyed the Harpy doctors on the other side of the glass.

"How is he?"

Phara's voice drew him to a halt and he sighed roughly. "Not well I fear," he whispered. He turned to block her view, holding her shoulders. "We got him here as fast as we could, but the wound is deep. Most likely, fatal."

Something strange flickered in his sister's eyes, a look he'd not seen since she'd first met Arin Manus some Suns past. Had she developed feelings for Tian? She couldn't have, not yet. It was too soon. But, who was he to judge. He'd fallen hard and fast for a human, a love that had only grown deeper the longer he spent with her. And nearly tore him apart when he'd thought he lost her.

Phara's questions coming out in a rush, breaking into his thoughts. "How? Who? Did you kill it?"

He gave her a squeeze, answering the best he could. "During the battle, one of the Orcs got too close. And yes, we killed it before we retreated."

Her jaw tightened and her spine stiffened. "Good." She paused, blinking back tears he knew she would never cry in front of him. "Can I see him?"

He jerked a thumb over his shoulder. "They are still working. Where is Lanni?"

She jerked a thumb toward the ceiling. "Resting, two floors up." Her hand came back down and landed on his chest. "Go. I can handle it."

He shook his head. As long as Lanni was safe, he'd go to her soon enough. Right now, Phara shouldn't be alone. Not that he worried she was too delicate for it or anything, but they were family and family stuck together. He moved aside so she could see into the ward and they waited.

And waited and waited some more.

Another six ticks passed before the Harpy's began to move away from the table one by one. He wasn't sure if that was bad, or good, but from Phara's soft gasp, it was probably bad.

One of the doctors came around, scrubbing his face with a long hand. He stopped in front of them, his wilted brown and blue feathers ruffling slightly in the air conditioning. The look on his face was grim, lines of worry pinching deep as he spoke in a low monotone. "Are you family?"

Phara sagged into his side as he replied. "Close enough, Doctor. What is wrong?"

He twisted a soaked cap between his fingers and tilted his head toward the glass. "We did what we could," he began. "But the wound was deep and the damage is extensive."

Phara shifted to see into the room herself and he caught the medics prepping Tian to be moved out of the corner of his eye.

"What is the prognosis?" he asked quietly, keeping one arm around his sister, just in case.

"The next rotation will decide." His feathered face turned toward Phara. "I am sorry," he added, reaching out to gently pat her upper arm.

She shook of the consoling gesture, glared at him and stomped down the hall. She paused at the doors and fell into step with the wheeled gurney as it rolled away.

He watched them disappear around a far corner and brought his gaze back to the poor Doctor. "Is there any hope?"

"I would not dare to say," he replied. "Chimera's are strong, yes, but the sword destroyed one of his hearts. We repaired it the best we could, but short of a miracle…"

***

He found them again, one flight above the trauma rooms and watched her from the doorway.

Phara paced alongside Tian's bed, fuming mad if the red hue on her cheeks was any indication. "You cannot die on me," she whispered vehemently. "I will not let you." She stopped long enough to stroke Tian's arm then resumed pacing. "You would not let me…"

The glitter on her cheeks broke his heart but there was nothing either of them could do. It would be up to the man himself. Giving the now humanoid-looking Tian a pitying glance, he whispered out a warning of his own. "Do not let my sister down."

With that said, he headed up to Lanni's room. Finding it just behind the nurse's rotunda, he paused for an update on her condition.

"She is resting," one of the secondary medics told him.

His heart jackhammered under his sternum and he allowed himself a moment of pure relief. When he'd seen her in the Undermarket, he feared he was too late and it almost sent him into the worst depression he'd ever thought could exist.

Entering her room, he paused for a heartbeat, still not liking the sickly paleness of her skin, or the too thin sight of her arms where they lay against the covers. Still, she was breathing on her own now, obviously aided along the road to recovery from the Spring Water he'd given her.

He quietly pulled the room's only chair beside the bed and gingerly picked up her frail hand. For all of two heartbeats, her bone-thin fingers lay limp against his palm, cold and still. Suddenly, they curled weakly against his. Lifting his gaze, he found her watching him through the small slits of her opened eyes.

Brushing a knuckle against her sunken cheek, he smiled. "Hello."

She leaned slowly into the caress and her lips lifted into a small smile, her reply not much more than a tiny croak. "Mithrin."

He knew then she'd be fine. She'd recognized him and that was all that mattered. Tears he didn't bother to deny himself, slipped free and slid down his cheeks.

"Well dammit all to hell and back. I can't leave you alone for a minute before you get yourself into all sorts of mischief."

He didn't recognize the voice, but Lanni did and her eyes widened, swinging to the door and the rather small woman standing there.

"Grams?" she croaked.

The older woman whirled into the room and bent over the bed to kiss Lanni's cheek. "I swear," she added, leaning her forehead against her granddaughter's for a long moment. "The trouble you girls cause..."

***

"So, he has another of your Blood Line?"

Draven's incredulous question filled the room and Diane's responding sniff actually set the monarch back a step. "Don't you take that tone with me," she snapped. "If your father had kept us in the loop..."

"My father's dead," Draven interrupted. "He never told me about you, or his promise. I found out after he died."

135

Tom watched his wife and the current, true King going head-to-head, as Dragon's do, over the communication stone they'd set up on the table of Lanni's room.

Fyris leaned against a nearby wall, the anxiousness in his eyes a telling sign that any moment he was likely to tear off back to Bra'ka.

Terra pushed Draven out of the frame a bit, her eyes falling on her sister and cutting off the argument. "I, I thought you were dead."

Lanni chuckled, coughed and shook her head. "Sorry," she managed to croak.

He could tell the sister's each wanted to say more, but Diana took the lead again, directing her next comment to her other granddaughter. "Bring me up to speed."

For the next hour, Terra explained all the events to date then Lanni told her side of things, as much as she could manage. Mithrin took over when she faltered and when they'd finished, both he and his wife let out low whistles.

But it was Diana that spoke, taking charge just like always. "It would seem we have several things in need of doing then, yes?" She lifted a hand and counted them off with raised fingers. "First would be to defend Gahroon. Second, we'll need to retake Rosau. Third, Fallon will need to be freed and finally, we'll need to oust Cannis and reclaim Bra'ka." Her silvery eyes passed over the group, including Draven and Terra. "Did I miss anything?"

The monarch and Terra shook their heads, along with Mithrin, Lanni and Fyris at her statements.

"So, what assets do we currently have? Who are

our allies?"

Draven ran a hand down his face. "The Cyclops, as you have seen, and the Chimera have agreed to fight with us. We still have the Dragon's and the few Goblins that survived the initial onslaught."

His wife turned toward Mithrin. "And the Naiad's? Is your father still bent on his dictates of non-involvement?"

Mithrin let out a sigh. "I fear so."

Diana snorted and muttered something under her breath in Draconic he didn't bother to translate. Neptune and the Dragons had never gotten along.

"Well then," she said, turning back to Draven. "You and Terra head to Gahroon. Rally the troops there. Torak and I will assemble the Dragon's here and send some your way to help. The rest will stay."

"How are you going to get past the shield?" Terra asked.

"The same way we got your sister out. You said there is an Orc inside yes? Along with your other friend?" Diana countered.

They both nodded but Mithrin interjected. "I do believe the Orc was the one that helped us escape. She took on several of the troops during the battle."

Diana turned to the Naiad. "Would you recognize her then?"

He shrugged. "It was dark, but I suppose."

His wife nodded decisively. "Good. Then you and Fyris will head into the city and find her. Get what information she has and work with it to find Fallon and bring down that shield."

When no one else said anything, she added, "We will attack in six days."

137

He asked his first question. "Why six love?"

Her pained eyes came back around to him. "Because that's the soonest the Unicorns can cast the spell again."

Fyris pushed off the wall, his entire body trembling. "How do you know?"

Diana moved around the end of the bed and laid a hand on his arm. "The black beasts need to recharge for one and second to that, that's how long it takes a Dragon Born to starve to death..."

***

Phara continued her pacing vigil, not sure what else to do with herself. She wanted to throw things, wanted to break things, *really* wanted to kill things.

But there was nothing to throw, even less to break and certainly no one readily available to kill...

How could this have happened?

Had Tian let his guard down? Was that how the Orc was able to sneak up on him? It had to be, but what caused him to be so careless?

Her maybe?

No, no, it couldn't be that. They barely knew each other. Hell, she had no idea who he was. Not really. There hadn't been a whole lot of time for talking.

Yet, here she was, drawn by something deep down in her soul to stay by his side. She couldn't explain it, didn't really want to analyze it.

She just had to be here.

Silent tears dropped from her jaw onto the blankets covering him.

Swiping them away, she slid to her knees. Picking

up one of the warm, strong hands that had so tenderly cared for *her*, she laid her other gently over the pristine white bandages covering one side of his chest.

And for the first time, ever in her long life, Phara Sylor wanted magic that could do more than make it rain...

Chapter Fifteen

"My, my, this is quite the mess you lot have gotten yourselves into."

As one, the group turned toward an ancient sounding voice. Leaning on her staff, the Crone Mother made her way into the room and gave everyone a look Lanni couldn't possibly read from her prone position.

Grams separated herself from Gramps and met the aged Harpy halfway. The two locked eyes and for a brief second something unspoken passed between them. The Crone nodded once, a crisp, decisive jerk and her wrinkled beak parted in a smile. Drawing Diana into a hug, her Grams disappeared into a cloud of white and brown feathers and she barely made out the words the old battle-axe whispered. "It is a good plan, M'Lady."

Diana stepped back, smiling herself and shrugged, as if they were discussing the weather and not the fate of the entire Five Kingdoms. "I know."

Speaking of weather...

She twisted toward the window, shuddering a bit as a deep, rumble of thunder rattled the pane. Lightning fractured the thick grey-blue surfaces rolling toward the building.

The Crone sighed, drawing her gaze away from the gathering storm and eyed Mithrin with a pinched glare. "Where is she..."

"One flight below," he answered, almost automatically.

"Who?" she asked.

He squeezed her fingers gently, a silent reprimand of sorts. She bristled but let it go as the bird-woman who'd saved her life, whirled and shuffled away, her thumping staff the only sound breaking the silence. She shook his hand, bringing his beautiful blue eyes back to hers. "Who is she talking about?"

He smiled and lifted their entwined fingers to give them a gentle kiss. "Phara."

She blinked. "Your sister is here?"

His response rumbling against the back of her hand. "She is down below with Tian."

Before she could reason that out, Grams clapped once. "Well, let's get this done. I'm not getting any younger." Her deep silver eyes landed on them and twinkled tenderly. "We'll give you a moment, Naiad. Don't dally."

Mithrin's breath huffed over her too thin skin. "Yes M'Lady."

Fyris, who looked eerily like Draven, Gramps and Grams left.

Mith's soulfully expressive eyes lifted, locking with hers. "Know that I do not wish to leave you."

She tightened her grip with all the strength she had. "I do. But, you're needed and I'm too weak to be of any help this time."

He shifted forward enough to splay her bony hand against his chest. "You help my heart. That is more than any other has ever done."

Tears pooled in his eyes and spilled over. Lifting her other hand, she wiped them away with shaking fingers.

Not that his imminent departure was causing that. Ok, it *was*, but it was also the weakness from nearly dying, *again*. She really needed to stop doing that, truly, it was getting old, real quick. She smiled, putting up a brave front and hoping he wouldn't see right through it.

141

He did, it was there in his eyes. To his credit, he kept it to himself. "I will come back to you."

She snorted. "You'd better. Otherwise, I'm gonna have to come find you and kick your ass."

He rose, laughing honestly and bent over the bed. His soft blue hair cascaded around her, pooling on the pillows. For just a heartbeat they were the only two beings in the entire Kingdom, hell the entire Universe.

She stared up into his eyes, praying to the God's above her affection for this man was visible.

His smile widened and his next whispered words set fire to her very soul. "I will hold you to that, Lanala Hortencia Heegan."

Where the hell he'd learned her full name, she'd never know. But spoken from *his* lips, it was the first time in her life, she didn't actually hate it. She searched his eyes, loving the tiny green specks swirling through the blue and put both hands on his cheeks. His natural, fresh musk, a combination of sea and sun, filled her lungs and she drew it deep, loving the tingle racing along her nerves like breaking waves on a sandy beach. She craved to feel his mouth on hers and slowly drew him closer, arms quaking with the strain of such a simple thing.

He got the hint. His face blurred, closing the gap and she expected a chaste, brush of his lips.

But that wasn't what she got. Not even close.

Despite her infirmity, he shifted his hands under her shoulders and sat back, drawing her off the bed and into his arms. They wrapped around her, digging into her hair and tilting her head just so.

She allowed it, too weak or unwilling, for that matter, to fight this man in any way. Hers came up, sliding around his shoulders and squeezed with everything she had to give.

His slightly scratchy tongue tickled across the seam of her mouth and she opened it on a sigh full of longing. He took the hint, again, and his tongue dove deep, roaming across the interior and the roof in a kiss she'd only dared to daydream of prior to now.

In her youth, on those days when she was all alone, she'd envisioned her perfect man, swooping in to whisk off her into the sunset. He'd gather her up and all her troubles would magically fade away.

Her mother's cruel verbal degradation, would be no more.

Her twins overshadowing perfectness, would dissipate in the brightness he created.

Her lonely existence would be filled with his love for her and her alone.

She'd had no idea what he looked like, or even that he'd be from another world entirely, but as they shared a kiss to end all kisses, her soul just knew, she'd finally found him...

Too soon, he pulled away and licked his lips, blue eyes glowing in the aftermath of their heated connection. A hand came up and wiped away tears she didn't realize she'd been crying. "Shhh, my love," he whispered, leaning his forehead to hers. "My heart will always bring me back to you."

She gulped, finding her voice and closed her eyes. "It'd better," she managed. "Cause right now, I honestly couldn't fight my way out of a wet paper bag."

***

143

After he'd gone, she lay there staring at the ceiling and doing her best to deny the self-pity and helplessness wanting to consume her. Fresh tears leaked out of the corner of her eyes, wetting her hair and rolling around her head to soak into the pillows.

"Enough of that."

She jerked at the command and struggled up on to an elbow.

The Crone whirled into the room for a second time, followed by a set of nurses pushing a bed. For just a breath, her heart stopped at the all too still figure it contained.

"Arin?"

The Harpy snorted and shook her head, feathers rustling. "Nay child. His kin."

The nurses maneuvered the bed around next to hers and the Crone slid into the chair Mithrin had recently vacated. She sighed heavily and waved away the others.

They left without a word and she rolled onto her side, biting back a groan. "Who is it?"

The older Harpy reached over and put a hand on the man's arm. "His name is Tian. And he needs our help."

Wait, wasn't he the one Mith's sister was with? He was.

She looked around for the other Naiad, but no one else entered the room. "Where's Phara?"

The Crone snorted softly. "She will only get in the way." The woman's pitch black eyes swung around and narrowed. "Are you ready?"

To do what? She could barely lift her head at the moment, but she still found herself nodding. "This is

144

going to hurt, isn't it..."

The gnarled staff lifted and slammed into floor.

She shifted enough to see over the edge of the bed, impressed when the wooden piece remained standing as the Crone's hand left it and landed on her cheek.

"Mayhap, a little..."

**

"Where are we?"

Lanni opened her eyes, spinning around to find the person who'd asked the question. A few feet away stood a man, no, wait a Chimera. He looked mostly human though but her heart knew him for what he was. "You must be Tian..."

His white haired head tilted. "I am. Who are you?"

Oh boy. That was a tough one. Was she human? Was she Dragon Born? What? She didn't know anymore. "I'm Lanni."

His white eyes pinched into a glare. "Do I know you?"

She chuckled. "No. You don't."

"Then, why are you here?"

She wondered that herself and looked around a bit more. The area was fuzzy, the images beyond him blurry. It reminded her a bit of her own coma like state when Tollo's purring had soothed her and she turned back to say as much but Tian had changed.

Gone was his humanoid self. He'd shifted and she admired his other half almost as much as she had Arin's. She'd heard of white lions in her world but they'd long ago become extinct, the last of them killed off by some poacher in 2021.

However, that's exactly what she was looking at now. A two-headed white lion of immense proportions. A good 8 feet at the shoulders, his manes glittered in the light coming from nowhere and everywhere. His horse flanks twitched and his blade tipped tail vibrated in agitation when she said nothing.

But it was his chest that drew her eye. She'd never known how Chimera physiology worked but she'd figured out from her interactions thus far, the brain split into both heads. The twin hearts Arin had mentioned had to follow suit.

A fact her gaze confirmed when some sort of filter or switch clicked on in her head. To date, she'd had no chance to explore whatever powers she'd inherited from Grams. Furiem had said she could commune with animals, which she'd already done many times. Handy, yes, but she'd yet to delve any deeper into it.

Apparently, communing also meant she could see right through them, like an x-ray. Which is what was happening at the moment. The filter showed his body in stark, glaring relief, including both hearts. The one on the right beat in double time, taking up the slack for its sluggish companion on the left.

She focused on the dark substance crushing around the struggling organ. It was a cancer trying to eat away at his flesh and blood.

"Do what you must child."

The Crone's order jolted her forward and without understanding what she was going to do, she drove her hand through the visible wound in his side.

He screamed, ok, more like roared.

146

"I'm sorry," she whispered. Wrapping her hand around the muscle, she cradled it, blocking off the darkness. "I have to do this."

He roared again, paws scraping and clawing at the ground.

She felt his agony and hissed when the toxin turned on her and began to sink into her hand. Tiny teeth tore at her flesh, but she refused to let go or move. It slithered up her arm, digging ever deeper as it crawled higher and higher.

She bent her head in determination, willing the poison to focus on her, see her for its next tasty meal, not Tian.

He roared a third time, resisting her and she put her other hand on his shoulder.

"Hold still," she bit out.

"*Tian? Tian? Stay with me, Tian*!"

Phara's desperate plea pierced into the dream state.

The Chimera stopped struggling, heads twisting this way and that. "Phara?" he called back, the name not much more than a soft croak.

She patted his shoulder. "That's right big guy, focus on her, not what I'm doing."

"*Tian?*" Phara called again, tears in her voice. "*Stay with me. Hold on, it is almost done...*"

She hoped that was right. She couldn't really be sure. The toxin was almost to her armpit now, coating hers in a slithering, writhing mass of black. She flipped the switch again, blinking to tighten in on the area around his dying heart. It looked clear and she slowly pulled back, curling her hand in to keep it all with her.

A step then two and she was ripped out of the

147

dream plane and back into the real world. Staggering away, she sagged against her own bed, Tian's blood dripping from the end of her hand. She had no idea when she'd gotten out of it, or why she had, but the Crone's firm voice helped to clear the fog.

"Quickly now, come child."

Phara stumbled around the end of the bed and fell to her knees. "Do it."

Without preamble, a white hot glow surrounded the Harpy's feather covered hand before it drove straight into Phara's chest.

The Naiad gasped, her eyes opening wide and her chest shrunk back out of reflex but she remained steady. Tears glittered on her lower lids and she snapped her mouth closed again, arching up to press against the Harpy's hand.

She reached out, Tian's blood dripping to the floor. "What the hell?"

"Shush! Let me work." The Crone's hand twisted in Phara's chest and their eyes remained locked with one another's. "*One together, one shall be. Love let live, souls to give.*"

She translated the clicks of the Harpy language in her head and smiled, slumping back to her own bed again. The Crone's hand withdrew, the white glow now tinged with red before it lifted toward Tian. The same clicks repeated and she slowly pressed it into the open, bleeding wound.

Until now, she hadn't realized the Chimera wasn't breathing, but the very second the Crone finished he arched off the covers and drew in a long, deep gasp.

Phara shot up, seemingly no worse for wear and bent over the bed, softly calling his name and stroking her hands over his face and chest.

Panting, the Harpy hunched in the chair.

She squatted next to her. "What did we do?"

The woman's beak parted in a slow grin and blood coated feathers patted her cheek. "Saved a very important life."

***

"So, Chimera can't live without both hearts? Is that what I'm getting?"

Alanna the Crone nodded, her eyes still pinched and haunted from whatever magic she'd worked earlier. "Correct." Her beak twisted toward the sleeping couple in the other bed. "One will keep them alive, the healthier of the two, but they cannot function without both."

"Did you give him Phara's then?"

Alanna stretched out her taloned feet and crossed them, for once speaking plainly. "In a way. Naiad's are very long lived. They do not age, as you think, for many, many Suns. In fact," she nodded toward the woman curled against the sleeping Chimera's side. "Her heart is the strongest I have ever felt. I simply took some of that and transferred it to him."

It sounded so simple, but she still didn't get her part in all of it. "So, what did I do?"

The Harpy blew out a long breath. "Decia's blood line always did have some very unique, quirks, for lack of better wording."

She frowned, scratching her cheek. "You mean I'm more than the Dragon version of Dr. Doolittle?"

Alanna actually laughed, a light, airy sound that

149

had her smiling too. "Yes. Each generation presents the quirks differently. Did you not ever wonder why you always wanted to fix the animals?" she asked after a pause.

She thought about that and realized she never had. As a kid, she'd considering becoming a Vet, of some sort, but then let it go when Terra went to University and she wasn't given the chance. Not that there was a whole lot of call for such things in her world, not anymore anyway, but still, she had wanted to help any injured animal she'd ever seen.

Alanna's beak tilted toward Tian. "At his core, his is an animal, yes?"

True. And put that way, what she'd done, removing the toxin made a weird sort of sense. "You put us in the dream so I wouldn't have to face what I was really doing."

Alanna's head bobbed. "It was easier, was it not?"

Chapter Sixteen

Fallon half-expected to be led into some deep, dark dungeon and thrown in.

But she wasn't. Instead, meat-head pressed the button for the 50th floor when they entered the elevator.

An inanely cheery music track filtered through the speakers and she worried briefly that she'd gone insane. Or, gotten herself trapped in Vid-land.

It wouldn't be the first time...

"Hey Trace? Mind pulling the plug for me?"

Meat-head snorted, shaking his head. "You're not on the Webs."

She shrugged. "Was worth a shot."

He grunted but said nothing more.

The elevator dinged and the doors parting on a soft hiss. Her escort took her arm and drug her down the hall. Pausing long enough to open a new door, he pushed her in and closed it.

Alone, she whistled softly. The suite was opulent to say the least. A long, low couch faced floor-to-ceiling windows, giving her a birds-eye view of the city beyond. Buildings of varying heights stared back, some with windows lit, but most were dark in the early evening. On the left wall, a large screen hung and a bookshelf had been carved into the right.

Just beyond the shelves, a hall curved away and she was tempted to explore it.

Later.

She was too tired and in just a bit of sensory overload. She needed to sit, let it all sink in and try to make some sense of it.

Making her way around the couch, she eased onto the cushions and put her head in her hands, her long, frizzy hair curtaining off the rest of the world.

What the hell had just happened?

One minute she was facing a swirling vortex of light and sound and the next she's on a rooftop, surrounded by *more* talking Unicorns.

One was bad enough, but five? Seriously?

And what was that green shield over the city?

She lifted her gaze to the windows again, just able to see the faint hue in the distance.

Who had put it there, more importantly why?

Was it to keep people in or out?

And where were Grams and Gramps? How did they relate to all this?

A brief flash of memory pierced through the questions zipping around in her grey matter like the computer code she loved.

When she'd caught a glimpse of them on the other side of the portal thingy, neither had seemed all that surprised at its presence, or the fact they were looking at a Unicorn...

"Would you like something to eat, or drink?"

She screeched at the question, more startled than scared because she hadn't heard anyone else in the place.

Searching she found a young, almost human looking woman standing at the end of the hall. A gossamer thin dress pooled around her feet and clung to a, well perfect body. Her waist was tiny, her shoulders slim and her arms long and gracefully sculpted. Her white-blond hair twisted about her chest and back in thick ringlets she'd have killed for in another

152

place and time.

There was something wrong though and the startling realization of what, jolted her past the fantasy of her looks. Around her neck, she wore a thick, heavy looking collar of gleaming metal that glowed with a faint aura of white-yellow. Attached to the front was a long chain that broke into a 'T' before stretching out to the left and right. It ended at a set of gleaming cuffs molded around each of her thin wrists.

She took a dainty step forward and another chain tinked against the floor. One eyebrow arched and she repeated her question. "Would her ladyship like something to eat, or drink?"

Ladyship? Wait, what?

"Um, no. I'm good. Who are you?"

She bowed deep, the chain almost scraping the floor in her servitude. "I am Azon." She straightened again, her red eyes dull and lackluster as she added, "How may I serve?"

Before she could answer, the door opened again and one of the Unicorns from the roof entered, followed by a creature she finally placed from Gramps tales as a Satyr. His hooves clomped across the room and he came around the couch, kicking out at Azon with a hard snort. "What are you still doing here? Should you not be below, seeing to the half-breed?"

Azon dropped to her knees with a rattle and she just barely caught the glint of defiance in her eyes before she demurely lowered them. "Yes Master. I was on my way…"

Her excuse was interrupted by his flank in her face, knocking her over. She grunted and Fallon almost shot off the couch to help but the Unicorns glare kept her

153

where she was.

He turned to his other minion, pawing at the floor. "See to the pet."

The goat-man helped Azon to her feet, leading her back out of the room.

"Forgive it," the Unicorn said, sounding almost sincere. "I hope she did not disturb you."

Hoping to keep the poor girl from getting into further trouble, she quickly shook her head. "She didn't."

A look of almost relief washed over his long face and he smiled. Which, a day ago, she'd have thought impossible, but there it was.

"Now, I suppose introductions would be in order, yes?"

Okay...this was going from weird to just plain creepy, in a hurry.

"I, erm, guess?"

The creature seemed pleased with her response and bowed back one of his front legs. "I am Lalam. Fifth of The Herd."

If that was supposed to mean something, it was lost on her. But, she shrugged and reciprocated. "Fallon Heegan, of the um, Boston Heegan's."

He rose, chuckling softly. "Oh my dear, you are so much more, are you not?"

She didn't have a clue what that meant either.

She was so out of her element here! Her fingers itched to be on her keyboards, her eyes craved to see her beloved screens scrolling with code, not Satyr's and Unicorns and women into kinky shit!

She was on the verge of saying just that when the Satyr and Azon reentered the room. The poor girl hobbled along, her previously dainty steps even more restricted now. Another chain had been attached between her hands and feet, pulling up on one and down on the other. The Satyr had even shoved a hard ball in her mouth.

She carried a small bucket in her hands and shuffled slowly toward the door.

"You forgot something pet," Lalam sneered.

The girl jolted and Fallon again tried to defend the poor thing. "Haven't you done enough?"

He whipped a dark glare her way and she snapped her mouth shut.

But it was the grateful look Azon twisted over her shoulder that changed her perception of the situation, very quickly. She was a prisoner too.

It didn't stop the Satyr from dropping a blindfold over her eyes, but still. The second jerking realization that the woman's position was no better than her own, sent a ripple of commiseration through her veins.

"Now, let us return to the topic at hand, yes?" Lalum said conversationally as Azon disappeared out the door.

Was he kidding?

He wasn't, sadly enough and she shifted back into the cushion.

If she'd learned one thing in her years as a hacker, information was power. And right now, she had none. Since Lalum seemed amiable enough, at least more so than Golix or Malice had, she might as well take advantage of it. "Alright, what can I do for you then?"

The creature paced in front of the windows, tail swishing with each clack of his hooves. "It is more what we can do for each other." He paused, red eyes coming

155

around to hers sharply. "You do know why you are here, yes?"

She shrugged. "I haven't the slightest clue."

His gaze narrowed. "You really do *not* know who you are, do you..."

It was a statement and another shrug lifted her shoulders into the air. "From the sounds of it, I guess not."

He laughed, a deep, full-bodied one that set her hackles on edge. Fire burned in her belly and she was tempted, briefly to let it out and just see what happened. She didn't, but the appeal was hard to resist.

He quieted and sighed then spoke as if to a child. "You, my dear, are Dragon Born. How could you *not* know that?"

She sat up. "Wait, what?"

He took a step forward, long neck curving gracefully as he bent to her eye-level. "Your grandparental is Decia Elfane, last remaining true Dragon of the Seventh House of Elfane."

She gulped, hard and everything in her life suddenly snapped into crystal clear focus. Just like it did when she was having problems with a particularly difficult hack or program, all of it abruptly made sense.

Her ability to breathe fire...

Her freaky strength...

Her uncanny hearing...

Her doubly freakish love of nearly burnt black meat...

Something else tickled at her thoughts. A conversation she'd overheard between Grams and Gramps when she was just a tot. It had been during one of the few times she'd visited the couple with her parents. She'd been playing, with what she couldn't remember now, but they'd stood in the doorway, talking in low voices she shouldn't have been able to hear.

But she had. Without having to strain at all.

She is the strongest yet, Grams had said.

Aye. Gramps agreed. *We shall have to keep a sharp eye on the lass.*

Ever after that, her parents refused to have anything to do with them and she'd always made the trip from Denver to Scotland on her own. Not that she minded, especially as she got older and more of her freakishness had come to light.

Her mother, though, had taken her to every doctor and specialist on the planet, trying to find some cure, or maybe it was a reason, for what she was. Of course, they all looked at dear old mom, like she was the crazy one, especially when Fallon refused to cooperate and prove her right by breathing fire or bending bars or whatever test it was they wanted her to complete.

Her parents had finally given up, not so much accepting her, but more ignoring her *condition*.

Which, in and of itself, was fine and dandy with her. The moment she could, she moved into her own place and buried herself deep in the world of computers...preferring the non-judgmental ones and zeros to anything and everything else.

And with the exception of Grams and Gramps, who mostly kept in touch through Vid helmets and her yearly visit to Scotland, she was happy being alone.

Until...

Shuddering at the thoughts of Byron Kelly IV, she blinked herself back and locked her gaze with the

Unicorn's again. "Well, I'll be damned."

The beast chuckled again and his red-eyes glowed with a power she couldn't place. "No, but you might be, if you do not take my deal..."

***

Fyris and Mithrin arrived on the outskirts of Bra'ka the following daylight. The sun leaked over the eastern skyline of the city, brightening the hue of the shield with reds and oranges.

The trip across the plains had been quiet, each man lost to his own thoughts and it was Fyris that broke the silence as he shifted down into humanoid form once they landed among the trees surrounding Cenna Lake. "Where should we start?"

Mithrin jerked a nod toward the shadowed pipe he'd crawled out of what seemed a lifetime ago. "The Undermarket. I am hopeful to find our Orc friend there. Or, at the very least, Manus."

The Dragon held out a hand. "After you then."

He sighed and they bent low, darting across the early morning shadows. The cool air stuck in his lungs, waiting for some alarm to sound at their approach, but they made the pipe without being spotted.

Crawling in, he tried not to smell the rotting water but it couldn't be helped. At least the trip this time was much faster without Lanni on his shoulder.

Fyris splashed along behind him, making enough racket to wake the dead.

He turned to censor the lug-head as they exited but a voice stopped him cold.

"Was wondering who was going to show up..."

He spun, hand falling to the sword at his waist then sighed in relief when the Orc they were looking for pushed off the nearby wall.

She held out a hand, her blue face cracking into a smile. "I do not think we had time for a formal introduction. I am Haydn Durel."

He took it. "Mithrin Sylor. A pleasure."

Fyris did the same.

"How is Lanni?" she asked immediately.

"Fine. Resting," he replied, a wide smile tugging across his lips at her name.

"Good to know." She turned, heading into the Market. "Follow me."

They did, weaving along the Caverns and catwalks almost to the other end where it entered up into the city proper. She turned down a tunnel and then into a small set of rooms before pausing.

Holding back a curtain and allowing them to go first, she whispered softly as he passed. "I am sorry for this. I do not have a choice…" She gulped, once. "Forgive me."

He caught her eye but was too late.

Ogres and Orcs came from everywhere, outnumbering them four to one.

Fyris roared and he could feel the man's fury and magic pulsing at the air. But there wasn't enough room to shift, not here, not without killing them all including himself and Haydn. Thankfully, the Dragon realized the folly of it and didn't morph into his true self.

But it didn't stop either of them from taking a few with…

They stood back to back in the center of the room, his sword swinging and cutting down any who came close.

Fyris used his bare hands, punching, tearing and ripping through any who got within reach.

But, in the end, it just wasn't enough...

Chapter Seventeen

"What in the Nether Worlds did you do *that* for?"

Haydn remained in the center of the boarding room, unmoved by the bellow from her lover. They'd taken refuge here while waiting for the others to arrive and she'd just spent the last tick explaining what had happened in the Market. Now his golden eyes spit fire as she replied in a calm tone. "It was the only way to get them inside The King's Tower, Arin."

His next roaring question rattled a dish centered on the coffee table so hard it slid across and bounced to the carpeting. "Did you at least warn them about this plan!?"

She sighed and tried to appease his anger. "There was no time."

His jaw flopped open. More fire blazed through his eyes and his next question pulsed with disbelief. "What, what if they had killed them outright?"

She shrugged. "I would not have let that happen. I am their commander. They had specific orders to bring them in alive."

"You...you..." He spun away, throwing up his hands. "How? You. What?"

She chewed on her inner cheek. It wasn't funny, in the slightest, but the mottled red on her love's face and his sputtering attempts to speak, were. She waited, patiently, until he stopped and stood, his frame shaking with anger. Walking across the room, she put a hand on his chest, his twin hearts pounding against her palm.

"Listen to me, *jaynan*," she began, using the pet name that always gained his attention. His eyes

161

focused, but his nostrils continued to flare in and out. "If I had warned them and they went along, even semi-willingly, the plan would not have worked. It needed to be real." She smiled softly. "An aside to that?"

He didn't respond to her question verbally but one eyebrow arched.

"They killed 20 before they went down..."

***

Fallon shifted against the wall, shivering a bit in the cold, dark room.

This is what she had expected in the beginning, not the opulent suite and the craziest deal anyone had ever offered her.

Yes, she was a hacker of some repute in her world. Ok, that wasn't true. She was *the* hacker. *The Firewall* and everyone, who was anyone, wanted her skills. They had for a long time now, she was that good. And they were willing to pay handsomely for what she could do too. She could admit it and without bragging about it.

But this...Lalum's plan was...insane! Pure, unaltered insanity!

Should she have taken him up on it though??

That was the real question. And one she hadn't a clue how to answer.

Even though he'd explained what he had in mind, she still didn't have enough information to make a rational decision.

At all.

The door opened on a creak and emitted a band of light into her otherwise black existence.

Two green skinned things she couldn't put a name

too dragged something in and unceremoniously released it.

A body thudded to the bitter stone and lay still.

One of the beasts grinned at her, his white teeth gleaming in the light and kicked the body in the ribs, hard.

He flopped over, groaning and she got a good look at him, her breath catching as she realized it was Fyris.

And he was one hell of a mess too.

His face was covered in cuts and gashes. One eye was swelling shut and the other wasn't much more than a shadow under the deep bruise forming around the socket. His cheeks were bloated and blood ran from both corners of his mouth. His nose looked to be broken and his jaw sported a long purpling welt along the edge. His shirt and pants hung in tatters and she spied several puncture wounds in his chest and stomach...

The Orc drew back his foot again and she thrust away from the wall, sliding to a halt over him. Before the blow could land, she belched a ball of white-hot fire and he swung right into it, unable to stop his own momentum.

An unlikely sense of satisfaction drummed along her nerves as he waved the melting appendage and staggered out of the cell. His screams rang off the walls and she chuckled, quirking an eyebrow at his companion.

The other swallowed, audibly and slowly, carefully backed into the hall.

The door shut and she spun, her eyes adjusting to the lack of light quickly. It was another handy trait she discovered soon after being tossed in the room and she knelt there, checking him over.

163

The worst of the wounds was a particularly deep slice across his side. Ripping a strip from his already destroyed shirt, she wadded it up and pressed it over the injury. It soaked through to quick and she pulled it away with a sickening slurp.

It continued to pump and she tore off another band. She had to stop it and a thought occurred to her. One she wouldn't have tried in her world, but if she didn't do something, he was going to bleed to death right in front of her eyes.

And she couldn't let that happen.

She wadded up the cloth and hiccupped twice to draw enough air into her gut to fuel the curse she'd lived with all her life. She held her breath, feeling the heat coil and twist in her belly. When she couldn't stand it any longer, she belched it back out. The flames caught the material and flared brightly. Closing her eyes, she slapped it over the damage. Nearly choking on the stench of burning flesh, she held it there, allowing it to cauterize the injury until she was satisfied it had sealed.

Sitting back, she blinked to clear the spots from her eyes and checked him over again, finding four more places in need of similar attention.

She looked to his face, thankful that he hadn't moved...yet.

Reaching up, she trailed a finger down his cheek, making a path through the blood and sighed. "Sorry there big guy, this is going to hurt...a lot."

***

Fyris' moan of pain echoed around the room, stirring her out of the semi-sleep state she'd drifted into. She sat up, stroking his blood coated hair.

His eyes blinked, well, one of them did, the other was even more swollen now than it had been when they tossed him in with her.

Which was another puzzle she'd tried to reason out during the hours after her impromptu surgery.

How did they know?

Why did they bring him here to her cell?

Had they seen him in the portal?

Or was it purely happenstance that they'd dumped him here?

Had Golix recaptured him in her world and then sent him back later?

So many questions and absolutely no answers, at least until he was awake...

With nothing better to do, she'd propped his head on her legs, leaned back and drifted off.

Now, that same head twisted her way slowly, a grimace on his distended, ugly features. Only he wasn't ugly. Even beaten, he was still the most handsome man she'd ever seen and her heart hammered to life under her ribs.

"Wh—where, are?"

It was about all he could seem to manage and she didn't blame the poor guy. He had to be hurting, above and beyond what she'd done to save his life. She smiled, stroking his temple which was probably the only part of him not marred in some way.

"You're safe."

Granted, it was an outright lie. They weren't safe at all. But the two words eased the flash of red in his eyes and that was enough, for now.

He drifted off again and she let him.

165

Answers could come later.

***

The next time he stirred her awake with a moan, she was the one blinking in shock. The high window was beginning to lighten with a new day and sunbeams cast across him in stark relief to the dark they'd last been in.

She expected him to look horrible, worse than before, but instead she found most of his injuries, the surface ones at least, already healed. The gash in his side and a few of the other, deeper ones she'd seared shut, still looked bad, but they too seemed to be knitting together nicely.

His eyes fluttered once, twice and a third time before opening fully. They shifted back and forth and a bright yellow oscillated across his irises. He inhaled sharply, nostrils flaring wide and before she could stop him, he shot off her lap with a bellow of anguish that nearly clawed her own soul right out of her body.

Mindlessly he slammed into the heavy door on the far side of the room. It groaned, creaked and for a second she thought it might cave in, but it held fast. He did it again and again and again, so many times she finally heard his shoulder betray him and dislocate with a rending crunch.

Cradling his arm, he turned to the room again, eyes electrified and glowing that same yellow she realized was outright panic. He drove his hand into his hair, gripping the side of his head so hard she thought for sure he'd squish his skull. When that failed, he whipped toward the wall and as he'd done back in Denver, began to grapple and paw at the stones.

He'd said nothing and she wasn't sure what to do to stop him. Scrambling back into the corner, she waited. He hadn't come out of it on his own back in the other building and as his nails broke against the walls, she knew he wouldn't do it here either.

It would be up to her.

But, she'd never dealt with anyone in an all-out panic attack before and she'd never bother to research the matter as she had so much else in her life behind a screen.

She wished she had now though...

He roared in frustration and resorted to punching the stones. The fracturing of his knuckles and heavy, growling breaths were the only sounds in the room, but each hit tore at her very essence.

The human part of her, wanted to curl up in a ball and stay out of his way.

But the Dragon side flared to life, opening to some instinct she couldn't put a name too if she wanted one.

It screamed in agony and when she couldn't stand it any longer, she gave into the intuition and let *that* guide her, instead of trying to use reason to help...

Forcing herself out of the corner, she bent low and when he paused for a breath, she rushed him, taking him down in a tangle of arms and legs.

He fought her and she was at long last thankful for her freakishly unaverage strength.

They rolled left...

They rolled right...

Each twist and turn accompanied by wild, mindless swings from him and not as quick ducks and weaves from her.

He caught her twice in the face, three or four times

167

in the ribs, but she wasn't giving up.

By the God's, if it took her last breath, she was going to snap him back to reality!

And then it hit her, smacked her right between the eyes like lightning actually and the next time she gained the upper hand, she pinned his good arm down with a knee, slammed both hands to either side of his head to hold him still and...

Kissed him.

***

Haydn meandered casually along the street. The sun had just crested the eastern side of the city and all around her, the citizens of Bra'ka moved along, their heads down and refusing to lift.

She couldn't blame them. If the situation were reversed and she wasn't a part of the invading army, she'd have tried to keep her head low too.

Oh, who was *she* kidding? She wouldn't. She'd have done exactly what she was doing. Fighting to fix it.

She shifted the small bag from one hand to the other, punching in the entry code she'd been given to the Tower. The door buzzed, opened and she slipped inside, hiding her smile for the cameras in the hall under a mask of bored indifference.

The Orc at the entrance, snapped to attention. "Commander!"

She grunted and gave his uniform, such as it was, a critical once over and barked out a dressing down for good measure.

The poor man remained rigid, eyes fixed beyond her shoulder and she stomped on down the hall when

168

she'd finished. It didn't make her happy to 'fall in line' with the enemy, but doing any less would have only brought suspicions on herself and they couldn't afford that.

Arin was still more than a little miffed over what she'd done the day before with the Dragon and the Naiad, but she'd assured him she would not let anything further happen.

The spontaneous plan, something she'd come up with on her way across the Market with the two of them in tow in fact, was the best viable option they had to get more people on the inside of this crazy mess.

In fact, it was probably the only one...

With them captured, Lalum and Cannis would undoubtedly think they'd won and relax. Which worked heavily in their favor.

Now, she just needed to find out what *their* plan was. Why they'd come to Bra'ka to begin with...

Surely they had one. She didn't think they'd risk it otherwise. Or, at least, Draven and Terra wouldn't let them do so without something more in the works.

Making her way down into the cells under the building, she stopped at the duty station. "Where are the prisoners they brought in last darkfall?"

The Ogre checked a board, answering without hesitation. "Cell fourteen and twenty-two, Commander."

She dropped the bag on his desk, opened it and pulled out a smaller rolled up set of 'tools'. Unrolling it, she tested the point of one with a nail, hiding her smile under the same mask of distain. "See that I am not disturbed."

The Ogre's eyes widened. "Yes, Commander."

Gathering up the equipment again, she spun sharply and headed off to cell fourteen first. Peeking through the window, she spied the Naiad, asleep in the far corner. He was unharmed, or at least no more than he had been in the fight and she moved on.

Cell twenty-two didn't have a window and she opened the door without preamble.

And found, a human and the Dragon...kissing. Heatedly kissing in fact and that snapped everything into focus.

Leaning against the jamb, she crossed her arms, chuckling. "I can return another time, if you like."

Chapter Eighteen

Fallon broke the kiss and looked up, blinking, at the blue-skinned female. "I'm sorry?"

The other woman shrugged, her tone unconcerned as she nodded toward Fyris. "I can give you some more time."

Now that...was just weird.

Was this woman friend, or foe?

She was standing there like a friend, but looked like the enemy. Save for the blue skin anyway. All the others she'd seen so far, were green.

Fyris answered the question for her. His head shifted toward the door and his previously yellow eyes blazed a brilliant red. "You!" he growled.

Bucking his chest, he nearly unseated her and she did the only thing she could think of.

She grabbed his face, pulled it back around...

And kissed him...again.

Only this time, unlike the last one, she put everything she had into it.

All the lonely nights in her loft back in Denver...

All the times she allowed herself just a moment to fantasize about *really* being loved...

All the cold winter days she'd stood gazing out her window, watching the couples stroll through the park hand in hand...

The fire she'd hated her entire life, corkscrewed through her gut, wriggling over and around itself with a thousand times more heat than she'd ever felt before. It contorted up her throat, hovering just at the back. It waited, smoldering against the roof of her mouth until

Fyris, once again distracted by her attentions, relaxed.

He quit trying to buck her off and his body went limp.

She eased the pressure on his working arm and it squirmed loose. He drove his hand into her hair and pulled back enough so she'd open her eyes again. His were clear now, back to the molten orange she knew.

He licked his lips, frowning in confusion. "*Kyleri*?"

She tried to gulp back the inferno to answer, couldn't and managed a slow nod.

"Your eyes...they are..."

She had no clue what he meant, which was more than a little annoying to be honest. She tried to swallow back the flames a second time, still couldn't and opened her mouth instead.

The woman at the door was forgotten, disappearing from that moment as if she'd never even existed.

His hand shifted from her hair to her jaw, curling around it with a protective gentleness she had only dreamed could exist in another person.

In that single instant, as they locked eyes, nothing else mattered.

They weren't in a cell...

Their future wasn't perilously close to ending before it even really began...

Their lives weren't balancing on some unknown factor...

It was just them.

Man and woman.

Dragon and Dragon Born.

With excruciating slowness, his head lifted off the floor and his lips claimed hers. The flames arched out of her mouth and into his. And for once, in all the years she'd been afflicted with this damnable oddity, it didn't burn. It was like a silky spring of softness that twirled from one being to another, engulfing them both in its embrace.

She shifted back in order to see his face. The flames continued to twist between them in a shower of sparks and light that would do a Fourth of July fireworks display right proud.

His lips were open, surprise in his eyes as he sucked the fire out of the air on a long breath.

She didn't think it ever would end, didn't want it too really, but it did. The last of the heat in her abdomen cooled and there was a moment that she actually missed its constant broiling, churning presence.

Fyris swallowed once, then again and with a powerful twist of his body, rolled them over. His rock hard erection drove into her belly and balancing on his good arm, he opened his mouth now.

At the back, a molten pool of red, orange and black swirled. It beckoned, calling her name on a whisper of smoke and heat. She brought both hands up, wrapping them around the nape of his neck with a fierce growl and took his lips.

She'd never been forward with a man.

Ever.

Hell, kissing Fyris was only the third time she'd ever had the experience. But, they say, '*third times the charm*...' and they, whoever that is, weren't wrong.

As it had from her to him, the inferno arched from one to the other and the Dragon side of her responded. Sucking the flames out of the air, she understood now, what he'd just gone through...

173

Four hundred years of memories is a lot to take in, all at once, but that's exactly what she got. As she lay there under him, everything he knew, everything he was, vibrated through her brain in a rush.

All the torment and torture he'd suffered under Golix...

All the doubt for his own sanity during the years after his escape...

All the anxiety and desperation he hid with sarcasm...

All the fear that he'd never find someone to see past the scars that littered his face and body...

And it was *the* most humbling event of her very short life.

Sharing your memories verbally with another is one thing, but living them as if they were your own, even in fast-forward, was almost overwhelming.

Almost.

Or, should have been for a normal human.

But, she wasn't normal and at long last, she was thankful for that.

The flames sputtered out and he collapsed against her, panting heavily in her ear. His hand slipped under her shoulder and he whispered two words so softly she almost missed them over the blood still pounding in her ears. "Thank you."

She cleared her throat, her reply shaky even as she stroked her hands down his back. "For?"

He lifted up and grinned that same cocky grin she remembered from their first meeting a lifetime ago, his eyes flickering between an amazing combination of blue and green. "Freeing me..."

The clearing of a throat echoed off the stone walls

of the cell. "Are you two done?"

***

"So, that is it? No grand Calvary coming to the rescue? No army to counter this one?

"I fear so," Fyris replied to the rush of questions. "If we are lucky, we will have 20 of my kin."

Fallon knew that to be an outright lie but kept it to herself. Fyris' distrust wavered around him, an aura she didn't have any difficulty deciphering. Whatever had happened between them, sealed them together and he'd become a beautifully open book to her eye.

His head thumped back against the wall and a wince danced across his face as she rubbed his shoulder. They'd popped it back in just moments ago, before the Orc, Haydn, had begun asking questions.

What had prompted Fyris to come to Bra'ka? What was the overall plan? Did Terra and Draven know? What did they need from her and Arin?

One after another they'd poured out and he'd answered each but she could tell he was holding back. She got it, especially with the memory of the Orc's seeming betrayal fresh in his mind and now in hers.

"Dragons or no," she said now. "That is not going to be enough."

Fyris other shoulder lifted in a slow shrug. "It will have to be."

Haydn's hand ran down her face. "When?"

"Soon," Fyris replied, glaring at her slightly when she pinched a nerve too hard.

She cocked a half smile. She'd never done this before, so he couldn't expect a masseuse or anything.

I was not, but ouch…

His voice in her head startled her and she inhaled sharply before she could stop herself.

Haydn noticed. "Are you well?"

She cut a look over her shoulder. "Fine. Just had a weird thought." She brought her eyes back to his. *Is this normal?*

His face remained impassive but she heard his chuckling response clear as day in her head. *When our kind True Mate? Yes.*

True Mate?

One corner of his mouth lifted slightly and his warm orange eyes shifted into that blue-green again. *I will explain…when we are alone.*

That sounded like an excellent idea to her and she cut another look at the Orc. "Since you're obviously on our side, can we get out of here now?"

Haydn squatted. "Not yet. If I free you, the forces will tear the city apart. It is better to stay here."

Fyris' jaw clenched and she felt him working it out before he finally nodded. "Agreed. Return for us in two rotations. Is the Naiad safe?"

She rose and headed for the door again. "He is. I will ensure you are not bothered as much as I can."

When the door had closed and locked again, she quirked an eyebrow up. *Care to explain all this?*

Pain shimmered through his eyes but he lifted his arm off her shoulder and cupped it around her face. His palm warmed her cheek and she held his gaze, his reply rippling through her mind.

Dragons seldom find their one True Mate, Kyleri. I spent 400 Suns seeking mine.

His thumb roamed her cheek and for just a

moment they shared all his old desperation and fears. It passed and he smiled, showing off that delectable dimple. Again, the undeniable urge to lick it consumed her thoughts, distracting her from what he was saying.

When we do though, the bond formed is complete and total.

How complete? How total? She asked.

His elbow folded, drawing her closer. *In all ways that matter. We are one in the same.*

That could have its advantages and its drawbacks. *Will you always know what I'm thinking?*

He nibbled at her lower lip, still smiling. *Mostly. I am sure we can learn to shutter it off. If we need too.*

She snickered, gave into the yearning and licked the crease in his cheek. *I expect you to teach me then. Cause, honestly, I'd prefer you* not *knowing everything sometimes.*

He shifted back and a possessive gleam rolled through his eyes. *I like the knowing.*

She sighed and brushed the longer locks of hair off his forehead. *Fine. But don't say I didn't warn you. I can go to some pretty dark places.*

His forehead touched hers and his eyes slipped closed. *You have already seen my darker side.* He pulled back again, all the old anguish plain as day on his face and in his eyes. *I am sorry, for earlier.*

She put a hand over his hearts, their beats drumming wildly against her palm. *I understand now. It was bad, wasn't it...*

It was a statement he didn't bother to deny. His memories played through her head, much slower this time and she wasn't sure if it was coming *from* him or just an effect of what they'd done earlier.

It got there. His words matched the recollections of that time and that place, like the voice over intro of a vid.

At first, they left me be. When they began to lose is when things got dark...

She embraced the moment, letting the flashback play out as it would.

She saw the first time they'd dragged him from a cell not unlike the one they were in now; felt his fear like a living thing even though he did his best to cover it with the bravado of youth...

She saw the new room where they took him, its blindingly white walls hurting her eyes even now where they prodded him with magic, forcing him to shift into his true self.

His speech continued, a dull, almost informative monotone all these years later, but she still caught the barest hint of a tremble underlying them.

Once I was exposed, they chained me to the floor and...began.

She felt every shock, every bolt as if she'd been there and sucked in a hard, angry breath. Her hand clutched into what remained of his shirt, twisting the material tight in her fist.

The rest of it sped up again becoming a blur of sights, sounds and screams. Time and time again, they yanked him from one cell to the other, forced him to shift and pinned him to the floor. They tortured him with all manner of spells and machines, asking the same questions over and over again.

How many are you?
How do we kill your kind?
What are your weaknesses?

It was the same three, nothing more. The sad part was, he didn't even know the answers. He was too young to have much knowledge of his kind and too far down the chain of command in the Wars going on to have that kind of Intel on his fellow troops...

But that didn't stop Golix and his fellow Unicorns from their perverse, sick games. When they figured out he'd give them nothing useful that's exactly what it became to them.

She could hear their laughter circulating just under his bellows of rage and pain.

She could hear the bets they started making as the days turned into weeks and then months and finally years.

How long would it be before he broke this time?

Would he just scream?

Would he just lay there?

Or would he growl and fight today?

When he became desensitized to the torture, they found new ways to make him react.

They cast spells, forcing him to hallucinate and see his mother, his friends, even other Dragons. They made him watch, believing through the magic that each of them had been captured and then killed right in front of him because he refused to talk.

He shuddered and his head dropping back to the wall with a thump that drew her out of the past.

She mirrored the tremor and eased her grip on his shirt. "I am so sorry," she whispered, meaning it with everything in her heart and soul.

His hand came up and wrapped around hers, squeezing tight as if he'd never let go again. "It was a long time ago."

179

Not to her! She'd just lived it and an anger she didn't even know she was capable of quaked through her body. She pounded him lightly in the chest. "I swear by all that's right and just, I will kill them all!"

Chapter Nineteen

"*Kyleri?* Come, you need to see this..."

Terra looked up from the battle plan she'd been working on at Draven's voice. He stood in the doorway to the office, a grim look on his face, yet strangely determined. She set aside the pencil and followed him back into the living area.

A Harpy she didn't recognize stood in front of the screen hanging on the wall, tapping one claw impatiently against his white lab coat. A flash of red and blue from his feathers caught the sunlight streaming in through the opened balcony door, ruffling them in the silence.

"What is it?" she asked.

The bird-like creature hit one of the buttons on the remote and the screen flickered to life, showing her a twisting band of colored strands. "We have determined what killed the Chimera..."

Ten minutes later, she had to stop him because everything was going right over her head. "Wait, just wait."

Reaching for the communication stone they'd used the day before, she connected it to Lanni in the Kyles medical center. "Hey sis," she said. "Listen to this..."

Setting the small device on the coffee table, she angled it so her twin could see and waved for the man to continue.

He cleared his throat, starting the presentation over. The screen first filled with one of the devices they'd confiscated from the *N'Val*. It was about three feet long and the outer shell glistened in the lighting from the lab where it had been examined. The image switched to an interior view of it, showing all the basic working parts of a bomb before it tightened in on the center portion. The illustration switched back to the lab and the Harpies in it, carefully opened it revealing twenty or so, long test tube looking things. Each glowed a weird, pulsing shade of bluish-green. One of the Harpies lifted one out and the picture switched to static before it was replaced by a split screen. On one side was a cell and the other held the spinning strand of DNA like material she'd seen when she first walked in.

"Well, yes, as I was saying. As you can see from our analysis of the device there are two distinct elements involved." The Harpy pointed to the picture on the left, confirming what she'd been thinking. "This is a standard cell. It is in you, me, all creatures."

The screen on the right widened out, filling the larger and he continued even as the DNA split into six different strands. "But this, this..." There was an excited tone to his voice and his pitch black eyes sparkled. "This is what, well. It is what we found inside the cells that is the most fascinating. As you can see it is a chain of material," he went on, pointing to each in turn. "This one here is Chimera. And here we have Dragon then Goblin then Harpy and then finally just a basic strand with no other distinctions." He pointed at the last in the line. "But here, here is what has us perplexed."

Lanni piped up, her eyes narrowing as she tapped a finger to her chin. "How so?"

The Harpy turned toward her. "We have never seen anything like it," he said honestly. "My fellow researchers have spent the last two rotations trying to match it to something in our datagroups, but we have come up empty feathered."

Her sister's eyes narrowed even further. "That's because it's not DNA."

One of the Harpy's bushy eyebrows lifted. "It is not? Then, what is it?"

"It's a virus."

Terra jerked, spinning toward her sister's face. "A virus? A DNA virus?"

Lanni chuckled sardonically. "No Terra, there is no such thing. It's a cold."

She blinked. "As in ah-choo-bless-me-I-feel-like-Dragon-Crap-On-A-Cracker cold?"

Lanni nodded slowly. "Unless I've forgotten the book I read on ancient infections, that's exactly what it is."

The Harpy interrupted. "What is a, cold?"

She explained it before Lanni could. "A hundred years ago, humans were plagued with many diseases. We had all sorts of cancers and viruses. We cured them as our technology evolved, but one of the worst we knew, was the common cold." She jerked a thumb at the screen. "It was a nasty little bugger that made you wish you were dead but you eventually got over it."

He blinked at her now, tilting his head in a very bird-like manner. "Is there a cure? Because that is ultimately what killed every citizen of Rosau and will likely kill all of us if there are any more of these things out there."

"What?" she and Lanni said together.

"That is what I was trying to point out." He looked to the screens again. "It has been engineered. This cold virus that you speak of..." He paused. "Nay, it is best to just show you." He huffed out a long breath and a video

183

began to play on the monitor. "During our inspection, one of my brothers was accidentally exposed."

In the playback, one of the Harpies, a rather tall looking male with black and green feathers, was bent over a table. He had several of the vials in a rack nearby and as he reached for something, it tipped over. One of the ampoule's rolled free and toward the edge of his workspace. He scrambled to catch it but missed. Almost in slow motion it fell, shattering on the floor.

Wide-eyed the poor creature backed away, heading for a secured looking door. Before he could reach it, the liquid reacted and a greenish cloud of smoke twisted into the air. It filled the environment quickly, blocking the camera's view for several seconds.

"We vented the chamber, but, we were too late..." The Harpy scientist explained in a very low, somber tone. When the scene cleared, the other Harpy lay in a heap his hand outstretched for the exit as blood, mucus and some sort of clear bodily fluid leaked from between his feathers. "It killed my Aerie Brother within a few heartbeats."

The vid cut out and Lanni spoke. "Wait, play that back."

The Scientist did as she asked, but didn't watch it again, the experience clearly painful for him.

She could hear Lanni's fingers snapping softly in the background as she spoke over it. "It's acting like...like, oh what was the name of that...Ebola! That's it. It's acting just the Ebola virus."

Terra well remembered the history lessons on the deadly disease that had decimated the populace of South Africa at one point many years ago. "How is that possible?"

Lanni's face frowned. "I'm not sure. Doctor? Can you send me what you have?"

His eyes narrowed at her sister. "Are you a scientist then?"

Lanni's responded with a smile and a twinkle in her eyes Terra hadn't seen in quite some time. "Heavens no. But I read a book once…"

Terra paced the balcony. She hated waiting. She really did. She'd always been very decisive. Give her a task and she was off and running. But this…

It was torture. She wanted to get going. Head for Gahroon and start putting her plans to action in order to defend the Butte's Arin and his kind called home. They knew from their scouts that the troops were still in Rosau, though what they were waiting for, she didn't know.

More ships loaded with bombs?

Maybe.

Given that they'd stopped the first attempt it was the most likely scenario. And, given the fact they hadn't heard from Haydn in some time now, she didn't know if the Orc had yet to find the factory, or do anything to stop production, so it was entirely possible that was exactly what they were doing. Either way, they needed to be on the Butte's if they wanted any chance at all of stopping another attack.

Draven appeared in the doorway, carrying the communication stone. He set it on the railing and activated it.

Lanni's face formed in the thick smoke. "Hey, listen, I think I might have figured out what Golix's end game is."

Draven sent her a confused look. "I thought we knew that. He wants control of the Rustac operations yes?"

Lanni sighed. "That was probably the initial goal, yes." She held up a piece of paper with a number of formulas and what looked like chicken scratch to her. "But, I don't think that's his final objective." She tapped the paper. "Not with this..."

"Sister dear, you know I've never been able to follow your scientific ramblings. Explain please."

Lanni laughed. "Fine. See, here's the thing..."

***

"She cannot be serious..." Draven said when Lanni had finished and the conference had been disconnected.

The look on his *Kyleri's* face though confirmed her sister was exactly that. "She is." She stepped forward and put a hand over his rapidly pounding hearts. "I'm sorry Draven, my love, but if you think about it, it does make perfect sense."

He threw up his hands and paced away. "But, how? Why? Why would he do such a thing? It is, it is, an extinction."

Terra held out a hand and he took it, grasping tightly to the life-line she was offering. "We knew there was more to this. Golix would not have gone to all this trouble, worked for so long for something so simple as just ruling your Kingdom. Would he?"

He scrubbed his free hand through his hair, massaging the back of his neck to stave off the building ache. "I, I do not know." He gulped, admitting something to her, he'd never said to anyone else. "My entire reign has been peaceful, *Kyleri*. Aside from the occasional territory dispute, there was not much to deal with." He tightened his fingers around hers. "I have no idea what I am doing here..."

She smiled, her eyes shifting from their normal silver to a light yellowish-green. "Neither do I, but I trust you and more importantly, I trust Lanni. If she says someone has genetically engineered those bombs to wipe out the various races who's DNA is in them, then I believe her."

He shuddered. "Do you think that is why he went to your world then? The real reason?"

She pulled him closer with their entwined fingers. She wrapped her arms around him and gave him a hard squeeze. "It makes the most sense. Though where he'd have found a copy of the common cold virus, I don't honestly know."

He buried his face in her hair, holding her tightly as a fear he'd never even dreamed of, settled around his three hearts. "Then what do we do?" he whispered against her neck.

"We stick with Grams plan. We defend Gahroon then head for Bra'ka to help take down that shield. It is the only way we will ever stop this..."

***

Lanni listened and watched the Harpies work. They'd asked her to join in on finding the counteragent, but she honestly didn't know what she could do. Still, she agreed. It was the least she could do for them sheltering Draven and Terra.

So, here she lay propped up in her bed in Kyles, observing the group around a long table. The scientists, like most, came in all shapes, sizes and feather colors and while she'd been introduced the day before, she couldn't remember a one of them now.

"What about sectar berries? They are acidic, yes?" one of them asked the room in general.

The one that had spoken to her sister the day before, slowly shook his head. "They are, but they are too few in number to be of value." His name was Zentai and despite being a bit snooty, he seemed like a nice enough sort overall. "And they are not in season."

One of them had theorized earlier, and she agreed, that destroying the goop in the vials before they could react with the atmosphere was their best option. By trial, error, and death, they'd found the catalyst for a reaction was the very air and nothing more. Though how that happened was beyond her.

In all the books she'd read over the years, she'd never heard of anything like it. Yes, there were airborne viruses, or had been back in the day. And she'd heard of more than a few that had mutated to transmit through the air, but none that *reacted* just because they were exposed to it.

It was a perplexing problem for sure.

They couldn't just blow the vials up. The day before, they'd tried it on one in the lab and while the container itself was destroyed, the goop remained.

They'd experimented with fire. It had melted the capsule, sure, quickly in fact, but the bluish-green goop seemed immune to the heat.

They'd attempted water next and had the same lack of results. The dastardly crap just floated to the

188

surface. It didn't react though, which was a possible solution. Limited yes, because it would just wash the stuff away, but still. She'd jotted down the idea anyway.

Earth didn't work any better either, the thinking being to just bury the stuff. They grabbed some dark, rich soil from somewhere, dug a hole and poured the contents in. When they dug it up just that morning, it had simply contaminated the clay.

Viable options is what they'd come together to discuss now.

Acid, or something similar sounded like an excellent answer, but there didn't seem to be anything in this world that would work.

Zentai turned toward the stone, directing a question to her. "Tell me, human, how did your kind solve this issue?"

It took a moment to figure out what he was asking. "Oh. Um, how did we cure the cold virus?"

"Yes, yes, that," he replied, snapping two talons together.

"In all honesty, we didn't. Not really anyway."

His feathered features pinched into a frown. "I do not understand."

She shrugged. "Well, if memory serves, someone developed...an...immunity..."

The clarity that the reason the goop worked so quickly here was because the creatures had absolutely no anti-bodies to counter it, hit her square between the eyes.

That was it!

The cold had never been cured in her world. They'd simply engineered a vaccine for it way back when and now every child was immunized at birth.

189

The creatures here had never been exposed, prior to now, unlike her kind that had lived with the virus for as long as anyone knew.

"I'll be right back..." She shut off the stone and bellowed one word. "Nurse!"

Chapter Twenty

"She succeeded!"

Terra looked up from the plans again and found Draven in the doorway.

"I'm sorry?"

"Lanni figured out a solution." He waved a hand. "Come, come."

Back in the main room, her sister's face hovered over the stone and Zentai turned at her entrance, a beaming smile on his beak. "Your human mirror is a genius."

Lanni snorted but she was smiling too. "I told you Zen, I'm not a genius."

She chuckled at her twin's modesty. "What'd you come up with?"

"The same vaccine we got as tots."

She snapped her fingers. "That's right. I forgot about that. Will it work?"

"The Harpies are replicating it, but it should," Lanni replied, her smile widening. "At least that's the theory."

She tilted a look at Zentai. "Can you do it?"

He nodded quickly, his feathers rustling. "Oh most definitely." He pointed at the flat screen on the wall. "It is simply a matter of combining your cure into the genetics of each race in question. Once that is complete, we can serve it up to all and it should counter the effects."

"Should?"

Zentai scratched at the feathers on his neck. "Yes, well, we will need a zero patient, but yes, should."

"I will do it."

She spun so quickly at those four words from Draven she nearly fell over. "What?! No! I won't let you. If, if it doesn't work, you'll die!"

He smiled patiently. "Doctor, please, give us a moment."

The Harpy bowed with a flourish and left.

Wordlessly, he shut off the stone, giving them some privacy.

Not that she cared if her sister overheard them but clearly he wanted it. She was still upset with him but it was more mild annoyance now than outright rage. Finding Lanni alive had helped but they'd yet to resolve the initial incident. At least, totally resolve it.

She loved him, of that there had never been a doubt, it was still trust at issue. Something he was about to rectify by the look in the molten orange of his eyes. He came across the living room and gently wrapped the strong hands she adored around her upper arms.

With a smile, he leaned his forehead to hers, his voice low. "You have done so much for me," he whispered. "For the Kingdoms that I can never even dream to repay it."

She put a hand on his chest. His heartbeat was a steady thump under her palm and she recognized the resolute look in his swirling eyes. "Draven…" She paused to swallow back the lump in her throat. "I didn't, I haven't," she stammered.

He put a single finger on her lips. "Shhhh, *Kyleri*, I know you did none of it for personal gain." His head pulled up, his eyes slowly roaming over her features. "That is what will make you an amazing Queen."

His warm fingers dropped back to her arm, stroking

up and down her flesh. As it always did, her body responded instantly to his touch. Blue-silver flames snapped to life and coiled around his hand, licking and caressing it with all the love she had to give.

His face shifted closer and he nuzzled her cheek, the next part a low rumble against the air. "I would be honored to have you stand in my stead."

She laughed nervously, hoping to lighten the moment. "Is that the Dragon version of a marriage proposal?"

His eyes slipped closed and he sighed. "If you are asking if I want to True Mate with you, nothing would make me happier," he whispered. "But, no. That is not what I was saying."

He stepped back, took both her hands and her heart tried to hammer its way right out of her chest.

"Terrina Decia Heegan, I decree that you are now inducted into House Taraxus," he said in the most formal, regal of tones. "I declare, as Ruler of the Third Kingdom of Gommel and Patriarch of the House, that you are hereby next in line to sit and adjudicate to all the needs of its citizens. Will you accept this honor and commit any and all Suns in your future to guiding the people firmly and fairly, should the need arise?"

She gulped hard and found her head dipping in a slow nod.

Draven's eyes flared a bright blue and a smile tugged at the corner of his lips. "You must answer, my love."

"I, I do?" she managed around the clog in her throat.

He cut a look over his shoulder toward the island between the living room and the kitchen. "Did you record that properly?"

"I did, Sire." Furiem's voice drifted across the silence. "You may sign when ready."

He let go of her, his shoulders set and spun around to scrawl his name on a piece of parchment the ferret was tapping with a feather tipped pen.

When he'd finished, the reporter rolled it up and tucked it under his arm, giving it a pat. "I will see this properly filed."

Draven laid the pen down and held out his hand. "Thank you. You have served my line well. I hope you will continue to do so."

Shock danced across the creatures face but he took one of Draven's fingers and shook it. "I will Your Majesty. You have my word."

And with that, he leapt off the counter and bounced through the door.

"What, just happened?"

He swung around again and entwined their fingers. "I merely protected the House," he whispered. "That way, if something happens, now or in the Suns to come, a Taraxian will rule."

She jerked back. "What?!"

He grabbed her firmly and pulled her against his chest. "No, no, love, it is merely a precaution."

She wanted to believe him, she really did, but the formality of the moment said it was much more. She squirmed her arms between them and shoved him back so she could see his face. "What did you do Draven?"

He cupped both hands around her cheeks and kissed her possessively.

As she always did, she melted, helpless to hold on to the flare of anger for long. There was something he wasn't saying, she could see it in his eyes but when his tongue tenderly rolled over the seam of her lips, the flames leapt to life, encircling them both in a haze of passion she was powerless to deny...

***

They made love after that but there was something different about it. Each time before, they'd come together full of passion, love and possession. This time, there was a sweetness, a tenderness to Draven she wasn't sure what to make of. Not that he'd ever been rough, no never that, but there was always an underlying current of desire she responded to in kind.

But now, as she lay curled against his side, sweaty and sated, she worried he was about to do something utterly stupid.

And she wasn't wrong...

***

An hour or so later, found them in one of the Harpy labs. A number of scientists had gathered, each with this world's version of a clipboard in hand and ready to make notes.

Draven sat on a stool, one sleeve rolled up to the shoulder.

"Are you sure about this, Your Majesty?" Zentai asked.

Her lover smiled, nodding. "As I can be. Are you?"

The Harpies reply was honest. "As we can be." He lifted a look to the others and one stepped forward, holding out a vial she recognized all too well.

195

Draven's strong hand wrapped around it but his eyes were on her. "Then we shall see what we see."

Zentai reached for a syringe on the table and stabbed him in the arm, depressing the plunger. "Give it ten heartbeats to work its way through your system."

His eyes never left hers. "Understood."

Her gut churned and twisted, sending acid up her neck.

He rose and walked toward the secured lab in which the other Harpy had perished. With a final look over his shoulder, he swung the door open and entered. It hissed shut in his wake and a red light over the other one switched to blue. He pushed that wide and strode into the room, his head high.

He didn't move but she counted with him. A full ten beats passed and he opened his hand. As it had done on the previous vid, time slowed as the vial twisted and spun over on itself before shattering on the tile like floor.

It had the same reaction and a cloud of green smoke enveloped him.

She jerked forward, pounding on the glass. "Draven!"

His hand appeared out of the cloud, landing on the other side with a solid thud.

"Vent the room!" she bellowed.

The area cleared and she found him, already on his knees, his chest expanding and contracting rapidly. His eyes came up and his fingers flexed against the barrier keeping them apart. He sank toward the floor, his face mottled in agony.

She dropped with him, tears streaming down hers. "Oh God's, baby, no..."

196

It wasn't working, that much was clear and she pushed off, grabbing the door and yanking with all her might. It didn't budge and she whirled, growling toward the scientists. "Open it! Let me in!"

Zentai jerked at her commands. "We, we cannot."

She punched the glass. It didn't break and she growled over her shoulder. "Open this now or I will pluck every one of you and make pillows!"

The door hissed and she yanked it wide. Stumbling over the threshold, she jerked the other one and caught Draven just as he tilted over. Blood, mucus and some other sort of fluid streamed down his cheeks, mingling with the tears dropping off her jaw.

"Oh God's baby," she whispered unevenly. She wiped his face with her sleeve, not caring she might be exposing herself to the deadly combination. "No, please, God's no."

A bloody hand came up to stroke her cheek and he blinked rapidly, his eyes dulling right in front of her. His chest expanded, contracted, expanded again and three words pushed past his lips. "I, love...you."

***

"It didn't work?"

The disbelief in her the young human's tone was understandable and Alanna nodded, leaning on her staff, her heart heavy with the news. "It did not."

Lanni picked up the sheaf of parchments she'd been laboring over for a rotation and a half. "I, I don't understand," she muttered. "I mean, I'm no scientist, but..." The writing utensil scratched across the paper. "And I carried the two, multiplied by four and..." She

197

continued like that for several tense moments before her eyes lifted, the silver surfaces filled with disappointment. "Who was it?"

She blinked. "I am sorry?"

"*Who* did the test?"

She had hoped to spare the girl but she'd asked and Alanna never lied. "His Majesty."

"What!?"

She winced in the face of that and sighed softly. "Draven tested the vaccine," she explained. "And it did not work."

The moment of anger passed and her eyes widened in shock. "Is, is he dead? Like the others?"

No use hiding it. "Yes."

Lanni's hand flew to her face, tears collecting in her eyes. "Oh dear Goddess..."

Chapter Twenty-One

"My Queen?"

The next morning found her curled up, utterly spent from a night of tears and pain.

He couldn't be gone. He couldn't. But there was absolutely no denying he'd drawn his last breath in her arms.

The scene replayed in her head, *again*, and fresh tears welled in her eyes.

"*Don't you leave me, you bastard! You can't. I won't let you…*"

His lungs rattled and even though she wasn't a doctor, she could tell they were rapidly filling with fluid. "*I am, sorry.*"

She shook her head, denying it despite the evidence he was dying right in front of her. "*You'll be fine. It'll work! It has too,*" she whispered vehemently. "*I can't, do this, alone.*"

One hand clutched weakly around hers. "*You, must. Rule, well, Kyleri. I, love, you.*"

And that was it.

One final, hard gasp for air and he was gone…

The scientists entered as soon as they dared and she knelt there, shock rippling across the limbs still wrapped around him. She blinked when Zentai squatted in front of her. "*What, what happened?*" she managed to ask.

His beak tilted down at Draven's lifeless corpse. "*I am unsure, but we will find out.*"

Before she could stop them, they lifted him away…

The tears had come later. After they'd tested her

and declared she was clean, she made her way back to the suite.

Furiem paced along the counter when she entered but she breezed past him and into their bedroom. Her eyes landed on the twisted sheets and she spun on a heel, unable to lay there with his smell still heavy on the air.

She'd chosen the other room and that's where the ferret found her now. Swiping back the water works, she answered in as strong a voice as she could muster. "What?"

He came around the bed, hopping up on the covers. "I am sorry," he said, patting her cheek. "But, there is news."

She eased the sheet back, snuffled once and rose, following him into the living room.

Zentai paced the floor, feather covered arms folded into the small of his back.

Lanni's pained features gazed at her through the stone and she spoke first. "Ter, I'm, I, don't know what to say."

She dismissed the apology with a shake of her head. She had every right to be angry, but not at her sister. "It was a risk," she said slowly. "I understood it." New tears coursed down her cheeks and her nose clogged, making her next words raspy and broken. "I'm not mad at you."

One hand lifted into the framed image and more than anything in the world, she wanted her twin close enough to fold into her arms and grieve.

But, she was on another continent and it couldn't be done.

Not right now.

Pulling her shoulders up, she put on the best front she could, turning toward Furiem and the Doctor. "You said there was news?"

Zentai stepped forward, a consolatory hand falling to her shoulder. "Yes. Well, we found what happened."

Tears tightening up her throat and she waved at him to get on with it.

Zentai's black eyes blinked. "Yes, well, His Majesties blood line carries an unusual, and before now, recessive gene. It reacted to the vaccine as the virus it is and blocked it off. We, should have tested," he paused.

The pain of failure was clear and she let him off the hook. "You had no way to know. Can we counter it?"

He nodded quickly. "Yes, we can modify it for the Taraxian line, M'Lady. It should not be a problem for future inoculations."

There was that word again. Should.

She wanted to clutch at it, rage at it even more, but she wasn't mad at him either.

What Draven had done was a risk, she'd felt it deep in her bones. And even though neither had voiced it, he'd known it too. It had been in his eyes right before he'd walked through that damn door...

Her vision blurred and she blinked, the water slipping down her cheeks.

From the Doc's explanation and the hurt on her twin's face, neither of them had seen this as a possible variable. Besides, it was done and there was nothing she could do to change the facts.

She smiled shakily at both and drew her shoulders up. "Good. Can we test the other races for a similar issue before we start mass production?"

Zentai bowed. "It is being done as we speak."

She gave Lanni another look. "Thank you. For your part in this."

Her twins face clouded with sadness. "Ter, I'm..."

She waved away a second apology, heaving out an angry growl into the air. "No, don't you dare. This isn't your fault, or mine. This belongs to one person, one creature and if it's the last thing I do, I will rip that golden horn off his head and shove it right up his ass!"

***

"He did what!?"

Lanni watched Grams face, saying it again as if that would make it less real. "Draven tested the vaccine on himself. He's, he's dead."

"Well, shit."

She couldn't agree more.

"How's Terra taking it?"

"As well as can be expected, I suppose." She huffed out a shaky breath. "Right before he, well, right before, he inducted her into the House and named her as heir. She's, taking over."

Grams face leaned away from the stone and she spoke to someone off camera. When she came back, there was a fire in her silver eyes that sent a skitter of fear down even her spine. "Very well. I'll spread the word. The others should reach Win-ra sometime later on today and they can head for Gahroon."

***

Under the cover of the next night, Terra led the

six Dragons Grams had sent across the desert. Strapped to their scales, were hundreds of drums containing the vaccine. Several Harpies held tight to her back but she ignored their digging claws. The liquid shifted and she was thankful that it kept her concentration on staying airborne instead of wallowing in a breaking heart.

They arrived well after midnight and she circled slowly, landing near Arin's house.

She desperately tried not to think about the last time she was here, with Draven and the moment he'd kissed her for the first time.

It honestly didn't work all that well and she could still feel his lips on hers...

She twisted away from the residence and scraped at a tear with her claw.

Thankfully, the Butte's were mostly empty, the Chimera having been evacuated by Draven's order before they'd downed the first ships. It'd been precautionary then but she was glad they'd stayed gone. There were enough remaining to help the Harpies efficiently unload the containers strapped across her back.

A reasonable guess was the main force would attack here, hoping to gain control of the mines themselves and further solidify their hold on the land. She wasn't going to take any more chances though and directed two of her team and their precious cargo to the other Butte's. "Lankor, please head to Dashta and make the delivery. Return here to help with defense when you're finished. Aco, head to Conbek and do the same."

Both of the massive beasts bowed their heads in respect. "Aye, My Queen."

She was *never* going to get used to that, so didn't bother with a response as they lifted off again, Harpies along for the ride.

When her scales were clear, she shifted back to a more comfortable size and set the troops to their tasks with a heavy heart.

It helped, occupying her time until the sun rose. She staggered into Arin's home and as she'd done in Win-ra avoided *the* room, choosing the one Lanni had been in oh so long ago.

And that's when she found her sister's note.

The single sheet was propped against the lamp on the bedside table and was as direct as the woman herself.

Sister dearest,

I'm alive. Just didn't want you to worry for me. I'm going after Arin. Be safe and for once let someone take care of you.
Love well and be happy...

Lanni.

When it had actually been left she had no way to know but could guess. And its implications brought fresh tears to her eyes, despite her exhaustion.

Shoulda, coulda, woulda scenario's raced through her thoughts, each bringing yet more tears for what could have been...

***

204

A rotation later, Carax stood proud on the bow of his new ship. The wind blew through his mane, lifting it behind him and he just knew today was going to be a good day! A perfect day, actually, as he'd get to see more of the two-headed ingrates writhe and perish under his assault.

The best part?

Like those in Rosau, they'd never know what hit them…

He cackled, the sound drifting away on the breeze rolling over the airborne ship. The vessels had arrived just that daylight, fully loaded with devices fresh off the production lines in Bra'ka and he couldn't wait to drop them.

"We are ready Master," one of the Orc's said beside him.

The Butte's were just coming into view, shadowed pillars rising out of the desert with grand majesty as the sun rose. Griffons circled the vessels, ready to provide support should any of the Chimera get lucky and be able to attack after the bomb run. And below, far enough behind to be unaffected by the virus after it reacted, was the rest of his Army.

Orc's and Ogre's packed the vehicles they'd confiscated in Rosau and the Centaurs galloped along the sand. Each of this troops was armed with bows and hundreds of poison tipped arrows.

Not that they would need them, but it was always best to be prepared.

The four ships eased within range and he nodded back to his minion. "At your pleasure, Captain."

The Orc turned. "Fire!"

Chapter Twenty-Two

Terra hid in the early morning shadows, not-so-patiently watching the sunlight settle over the ships hovering above Gahroon.

It was the moment of truth. All the work, the preparation had come down to this.

They'd vaccinated everyone here, from the Dragons, to the Chimera and the few Goblins that had tagged along with her and Draven during their retreat from Bra'ka.

All the non-essential personnel had been evacuated, leaving just the Warriors of the 1st and 2nd Prides, her and the six Dragons.

They'd spent the day before shoring up the defenses around the Butte's.

They'd added a weird sort of barbed wire to the edges of each...

They'd slicked down the sides of the tall, rocky pillars with some of the greasy water residue that no one had ever bothered to name and was left over after the Rustac ore was mined from the ground...

They'd coated the bridges between the outcroppings of clay and rock with Rustac dust, the highly volatile compound that remained after the ore was processed and once lit, would explode into a raging firestorm sure to incinerate anything in its path...

All in all, Gahroon was as defended as it was going to get.

So why did she feel like she'd missed something?

Scanning the hidden troops close by, she willed whatever was nagging at her to stand up and smack her.

But, it didn't.

Instead, the next sound to pierce the daylight was the whine of hydraulics as the bomb bay doors cracked and began to open above them...

***

Carax leaned over the rail, flanks shivering as the first of the devices released and sailed toward the ground with high-pitched whistles.

It hit, aimed perfectly and exploded like it was supposed to. The next followed and the next and the next, each of them kicking up a small plume of reddish-brown dust before the deadly green clouds overshadowed it.

He danced on his hooves, ears cocked forward as the vapor enveloped and invaded the homes and businesses below, and anticipated the torment to come.

But nothing happened.

There were no screams...no cries for help...no, nothing.

He leaned further over the rail, scanning the landscape as the toxic fog began to clear.

Again, he found nothing. No bodies, no horrifically disfigured corpses...nothing.

How could that be? There should be hundreds of thousands fleeing his invention.

They should be terrorized, traumatized by the lethal gasses he'd unleashed!

"Now!"

The command bellowed across the early daylight and he backed up a single step, horrified as the terrain filled with Chimera's and Dragons!

They shot into the air, wings flapping loudly as they descended on his ships.

***

"On the left!"

"Watch the right!"

"Down below!"

"From above and right..."

The stone tucked under a scale near her ear crackled with the ongoing combat and she smiled. Spinning on a wing, she came back around for another pass at the lead ship.

Belching out a blast of fire, it consumed the front deck quickly, melting it right out from under the Unicorn's hooves.

"You bitch! How?!" he screamed, dancing away from the flames.

She spun under the craft, coming up to hover close to the starboard side. "We're immune you donkey's ass!" she called back, smiling for the first time in days. "Will you yield?"

"Never!" he raged. He pawed at the metal and lowered his head, backing up the denial with a series of rapid fire magic bolts shooting from his glowing horn.

She dodged them, catching only one in the side. She came back around, hovering again, taunting him. "You're going to lose! Surrender and I might let you live..."

There was a slight lull in the chatter near her ear and she listened to the static before he could answer.

"On the ground!"

The beast cackled as a swath of arrows sailed up from the ground. Something, or someone slammed into her side, shifting her out of the way. One creased the scales along her tail and she bellowed in pain, the Unicorn temporarily forgotten.

"To me," she called across the stone.

Five of the six other Dragons fell into a formation on her tail and they plummeted toward the sand. Dragging the dry air into her lungs, she let it broil through her gut. Fueled by rage for Draven, she strafed the troops rolling up to the base of the rocky towers, feeling absolutely no remorse for the incinerated troops she left behind...

***

The Dragon bitch dropped out of sight and he took stock.

The Griffons he'd brought along for support were engaged in lethal combat with the Chimera's. And at a two-to-one ratio, they were rapidly losing the upper hand he should have had.

Two of his four ships were already gone, nothing more than smoldering piles of metal now. The third was teetering in the air, in danger of going down at any heartbeat. And his? The fire had been put out, but the deck was torched, a giant hole showing him the cargo area under it.

And things weren't going much better on the ground.

Sidling up to the rail, he leaned out and bellowed new orders. "Retreat! Fall back you fools!"

They were too far up in the air for them to be

heard and he spun toward the Captain, repeating the commands. "Go! Go! Get us out of here!"

The Orc snapped off a smart salute and headed for the bridge.

***

Terra caught the retreating vessel out of the corner of her eye. "Regroup."

The Dragons disengaged from their strafing runs and came around to her.

She pointed toward the ship with the tilt of a wing. "He can't get away. Aco, take out the engines. Lankor, Zula, with me. The rest of you, continue to keep them occupied."

The four shot away from their impromptu meeting, dive bombing the troops. The Chimera finished off the last of the Griffons and joined in the fray, creating the chaos she was hoping for.

Twirling, she aimed for the smoking remains of Carax's airboat. As directed, Aco landed on the stern, his claws ripping into the metal to get at the turbines. Lankor and Zula flew around, bombarding the starboard and port sides with fireball after fireball. She headed for the bow, searching for the Unicorn.

He stood there, as smug as ever, his horn tip luminous. "I will not be denied!"

"You've already lost. Surrender now!"

"Never. This is only beginning Dragon."

She inhaled a burst of hot air, dragging it deep and fired off at the same time his horn shot a beam of light off the deck. Her muscles coiled tight, ready to dodge it but it wasn't aimed at her.

210

Instead, it pooled a few feet off the deck and solidified into a portal, Bra'ka's skyline just visible in the fuzzy image.

She didn't know a single Unicorn was capable of such things, but this particular beast was stronger than she'd given him credit for. She didn't recognize him as one of the five she'd already met, but Mithrin had said there were at least eight in the Herd.

A cackle slithered across the air and his hooves rang on the metal as he galloped for the bow.

She fired the blast in her gut, narrowly missing his flashing hooves as they pushed him clear of the railing.

She flapped her wings hard, catching a burst of air and opened her maw to snatch him from the sky.

But, she missed and he disappeared through the shimmering surface...

***

"How could you let this happen?"

Cannis shifted from one foot to the other. "Um, Master, it was not intentional. We..."

Carax stepped in front of him, smoke still wafting off parts of his body. "Father. They have developed an immunity."

Golix's face jerked in the cloudy image of the stone. "What!? How could you let this happen?" he said for a second time.

Carax snorted and pawed at the marble floor of the throne room. "*I* let nothing happen. This was *your* plan. How was I to know they would get a hold of one of the devices? How did *you* not see this coming?"

Azon listened intently from the corner of the room.

Even with her head down, there was no way to miss the argument or the anger of those involved. Her father and brother had never gotten along, so it was no surprise Carax was standing up for himself.

She toyed with the links keeping her hands pinned to her waist, wishing there was enough slack in her chains to get at the gag covering her lips. She'd love to be free to speak...and gloat that all her father's planning and scheming was failing miserably.

But she wasn't and had to satisfy herself with a smirk under the leather.

Lalum, who'd brought her up here to detail her slights to Golix during their daily communication, kicked back at her, hissing. "Get out. Go, see to the half-breed."

She dodged the blow, letting it glance off her arm instead of her chest. She pushed to her feet and shuffled toward the door, hoping to avoid her father's ire for yet another rotation.

But the God's had never liked her and Golix interrupted his own tirade. "Is that my other spawn?"

She froze mid-step and hung her head.

Lalum stepped out of the shadows he'd been hiding in, coming between them as she turned, his reply was full of due reverence. "It is, Master."

"What is she doing here?"

Her captor's hooves clacked against the marble. "I brought her up. To keep an eye upon her."

She moved enough to see him around Lalum's quivering flank, sighing through her nose.

"Are those chains ensuring her behavior?"

Lalum's head dropped. "Indeed. She has been the perfect pet."

Golix snorted loudly. "Somehow I doubt that." His good eye narrowed toward her. "Are you enjoying yourself, daughter?"

It was a rhetorical question, one that he asked consistently, knowing damn good and well she hated him and what he'd done to her a hundred Suns before. But, this rotation, she nodded slowly, keeping her eyes pinned firmly to the floor. She was so close to finally being free of this wretched family that she wasn't about to risk it.

She felt his eye shift back to Lalum and let out a mental sigh of relief.

"See that she continues to have no freedom, per our agreement."

Lalum's tail swished her way and she spun, resuming her path to the exit but not before hearing his reply. "Aye, Master. I will keep her enchained until you say otherwise…"

In the elevator and on her way to the dungeons, Azon gave into the rage and struggled at her bonds. She yanked and pulled, twisted and squirmed, trying, hoping something might finally give.

But, as always, the moment she put any effort into being free of the cuffs her own father had ordered Lalum to seal around her skin, they glowed in reaction. With each scrape of her nails, tug of her arms or kick of her feet, they shocked her with ever increasing power. She howled into her gag, both angry and hurt and finally had to give up or risk passing out from the pain.

Kneeling, she panted through her nose, wishing she still had her own magic. Maybe with that, she could counter the spells around the chains and the one her

213

father had cast to keep her in this form.

She longed to run free, feel the wind in her mane, feel the grass of home under her hooves...

A single tear leaked out of her eye and she could do nothing to stop it from trailing down her cheek. Which was the worst part. She could deal with being humanoid, she had had no problem shifting between one and the other when she was younger.

But these...

She gave the magically enhanced metal another tug and received another shock for her trouble. She hated the restriction, even a hundred Suns later.

The elevator dinged and she shuffled through the doors as soon as there was enough space. Excitement tingled across her nerves as she hobbled down the hall and spied the blue-skinned Commander on duty.

She was hoping for this. Seeing Rygan after she passed along this latest intel would just be a bonus.

Shambling up to the desk, the Orc rose and came around, a smile in her red-blue eyes. She slipped her hands behind her neck and discretely undid the gag.

She licked her lips and whispered her message quickly. "They failed in Gahroon. Carax has returned to Bra'ka."

Commander Durel's eyes sparkled even as she stepped away to head back to her seat. "Good news," she replied in a low voice. Her chin tilted slightly toward a room off to their left. "He is better."

Another burst of elation tripped across her chest. "Thank you."

Keeping her back to the camera, she plodded to his cell and shouldered open the door when it buzzed to release.

Stretched tight to a cross hung on the wall, Rygan's eyes lit up as she tottered across the room. Sadly, it was the only part of him he could move and she carefully checked his wings, noting several of the feathers were starting to come back in.

He might even be able to fly again, one day...

Leaning her cheek against his chest, she sighed softly. "We will be free," she whispered. "Soon."

Air expanded the skin under her face, at least as much as the straps holding him up allowed and she mirrored the response. She gently touched his thigh, as high as she could reach and tilted a look up. Water pooled in his eyes and she stroked her fingers along the muscles of his leg.

"Soon," she said again. "Very soon."

Chapter Twenty-Three

Diana walked the ridge of the hill, pausing to stare down at the city for a moment then resumed her vigil. Flapping wings disturbed her hair and she turned in time to see another of her kin land in the valley on the other side.

They'd arrived from Kyles and taken up position north of the metropolis. It wasn't the exact spot Draven and Terra had attacked from the first time, but it was close. Behind her, a number of Dragons had already arrived and she heard more coming.

The few who could, had shifted down into their humanoid versions, but most of the beasts were large enough that they'd draw attention come the next daylight.

That was ok. She wanted it. She needed Cannis and the remaining Unicorns focused on her and her kind. The more of the invaders they could draw out, the better chance the others would have.

One of them now, separated himself and strode confidently up the hill, strapping weapons and equipment to the twin bandoliers crossed over his shoulders. His bald head caught the moonlight, shining like a beacon in the darkness and the bright orange-red eyes typical of their kind, swept over her. He stopped beside her and bowed at the waist. "M'Lady. How may I be of service?"

She smiled at the younger man. "My sources tell me you are the best at infiltration. Is this true?"

He shifted the weapons on his chest. "It may be. What do you need?"

She hitched a thumb toward the city in the distance. "There is a warehouse in there. I want it leveled."

He tilted his head in a nod of acknowledgment. "Where?"

She rattled off the information and the importance of ensuring the virus did not get out into the open.

He bowed again. "Consider it done." He started down the hill, melding into the deep shadows cast by the trees until she lost sight of him completely.

"Are you ready?"

At Tom's question, she set her shoulders. "I suppose." He drew her around, clasping his hands in the small of her back. She stared up into his eyes, cupping an aged hand around his cheek. "We have had a good life husband. Any regrets?"

He cocked that Scottish smile she'd fallen in love with a thousand years ago. "Not a one, lass. You?"

She chuckled and laid her head against his chest. "Save for the fact I never could get you to quit snoring?"

His laugh rumbled under her ear but anything he would have said was interrupted by more flapping wings above.

She tilted a look up and sighed. "Time to go to work my love."

***

Azon wanted to stay longer, but she didn't dare. There were chores to do and intel to gather yet and she wasn't above helping, if it meant they'd all be able to escape. With a last nuzzle of Rygan's chest, she gave it quick kiss and shuffled back to the door.

217

Giving it a kick, it buzzed and opened a crack. Haydn greeted her and kept her in the archway, replacing the gag out of the camera's view. When she turned the corner to go back to the elevator, everything was as it should be...

Arriving at the door to their suite, it yanked open before she could reach the handle.

On the other side was one of her worst nightmares. A Satyr by the name of Cunka, who took way to much pleasure in her misery. His tiny, beady eyes roamed up and down and a smirk crossed his lips. "The Master said you have been bad, girlie," he hissed. "And need to be punished..."

Fear shivered down her spine and she tried to run, but he caught her within a few steps and dragged her back, despite her screaming pleas.

Pulling her along by the hair, he shoved her into the small, almost closet like area they'd given her to sleep and pushed her down on the bare mattress in the corner.

She kicked and rolled, anticipating the worst, but Lalum would never allow anyone that pleasure.

Instead, Cunka shoved a rod under her arms, drawing them back at the elbows. Pulling her feet up, he tied them off to it, pulling the rope tight to bow her nearly in half. He removed the gag and she tried to plead with him, but he silenced her with more rope. Looping several coils between her lips and tied it off at her back, again, pulling it so tight she had no choice but to stare straight ahead.

Finished, he bent close to her ear and hissed out the two words she'd been dreading since she started passing information along to the Orc. "They know..."

218

***

The stone Haydn had hidden under some paperwork buzzed. Sliding it free, she kept it out of the view of the camera over her shoulder and turned it on.

The young woman's face appeared in the smoke and she hissed out a warning. "Get out. They know."

Without waiting for more, she dropped it and crushed it under a boot heel. Pulling the keyboard close, she tapped in a command, activating the program the human had scratched out on a piece of paper the day before and she'd retyped at the start of her shift.

Kicking her booted feet up on the desk, a smile crossed her lips. Her spirits lifted and she laughed as the virus worm, whatever that was, clawed its way through the limited computerized system in the building, crashing everything.

Doors up and down the hallway buzzed and cracked releasing the prisoners one by one.

She couldn't care less about any of them and clasped her hands behind her head. "Oh, help," she said, her voice a dull monotone. "They are getting away."

Fallon slid to a halt next to the desk, the Dragon on her heels. "What are you doing?"

She laughed. "Trying to get up the energy to stop you..."

The human's eyes rolled. "Come on, we're not leaving you behind."

Haydn pushed back and headed for Rygan's cell. "I have no intention of staying." She shoved open the door and started undoing the straps holding the half-ogre, half-harpy on the cross. She'd promised Azon she'd take him along when the time came and she wasn't about to go back on her word.

He flopped free, unable to stand on his own and weakly whispered a name. "Azon..."

She threw his arm over her shoulder and hitched the other around his waist. "I know big guy. Do not worry, I will see to her."

She met up again with Fallon, Fyris and the Naiad, whose name she didn't know and herded them toward the stairs.

"Azon..." Rygan whispered again.

"Who's that?" Fallon asked.

"She has been passing me intel," Haydn replied as they started up. "She is a captive of Lalum."

Fallon drew up short. "You mean that blonde girl?"

"Yes."

"Shit. Well, we can't leave her." She gazed at the Dragon. "Fy, we have to help."

They all paused on the landing between the dungeon and lobby levels and she sighed. Handing off the Half-Orge to the Naiad, she took command. "Very well, you two come with me. Naiad, take him to 222 Losten Paved. Knock four times and wait. Four times, any more and you will be met with a very angry Chimera. Understand?"

***

Six flights later, Fallon paused, bending over to catch her breath. "Wait, wait," she panted. "Isn't there an easier way?"

Haydn kept one foot on the step above. "If we had

control of the building, maybe."

She straightened at that, grinning widely. "There's a control room?"

The Orc's thumb jerked up. "Two flights away. Why?"

Reinvigorated, she took the stairs two at a time the rest of the way. "Oh yeah baby. Bring it on!"

It took her lover and the Orc less time than she would have thought to dispatch the three Ogre's and four Orc's manning the room and her smile widened. Spinning into the chair, she cracked her knuckles. "Alright, let's see what's what..."

She bypassed a security code she'd first hacked when she was five and laid into the guts of the system. In short order, she had a bird's eye view of what was happening, both inside and outside the building.

Outside, on the streets, troops were rushing here and there, obviously gearing up for something.

"Is Grams attacking?"

"Switch to the view beyond the shield."

She pulled up the feeds and sure enough, a massive force of Dragons, Griffons and Centaurs had already engaged one another in the fields and air surrounding Bra'ka. On the ground, the Ogre's and Orc's were marching steadily toward the chaos, easily outnumbering Grams forces.

She punched up the communication system, listening to the chatter.

"Attack!" someone who sounded suspiciously like Lalum ordered.

The Ogre's and Orc's surged forward and an idea occurred to her. Her fingers flew across the keys and she explained while she worked to divert the comm signal. "When this is done, I want you to take control of the troops Orc."

"What?"

She spun the chair enough to see the woman's face. "You heard me," she turned back and kept typing. "Make them stop, do the hokey pokey, or dance a jig, I could care less."

Haydn's laugh was infectious and she finished off the hack. The room filled with a screech and the Orc stepped to the mic, cleared her throat and spoke.

"Regiment four, hold the line. Regiment two, flank left. Regiment six, flank right."

Thank the God's, Orc's and Ogre's were very literal.

On the screens, about 200 of the army on the left suddenly turned and smashed into their fellows in the middle who'd just as suddenly stopped dead and remained unmoving. On the right side of the screen, another 200 did the same and the chaos that followed was a beautiful thing.

Ogre and Orc alike crashed over and through one another, some being trampled under the boots of their fellow soldiers. And yet more just stood there, clearly confused as to what they were supposed to be doing, especially when their Orc added more orders to the fray.

"Regiment three, all members of regiment two have been declared traitors," Haydn said in her best official sounding voice. "Regiment one, all members of regiment seven have been declared spies for the Dragons..." She gave several more orders of a similar nature until every troop in the field seem to think every other troop was against them.

The Orc stepped back from the mic, nodding. "That

should keep them occupied for some time I believe."

She laughed and sent the program she'd written in the interim through the system, further locking it up. "Ok, let's go get the girl..."

Several floors later, Fyris kicked open the door to the suite she'd been in when she first arrived. The same place where Lalum had tried to convert her to their side in this mess. "Where is she?"

Haydn headed for the hallway she'd never had a chance to explore. Rounding the corner, she opened the door to a small room and found Azon face down on a thin mattress.

Freeing her, Fyris tried to break the chains but the poor thing screamed in agony the minute there was any pressure put to the links. "No, no. It is fine. We need to go."

"What's the best way?"

"The roof," The girl panted as Fyris scooped her into his arms.

"Can we do that?" she asked. "With the shield?"

Fyris shrugged. "I can at least get us off the building," he offered. "I am a Dragon after all."

***

Diana watched the pandemonium ensue from her vantage point and knew now was as good a time as any.

Twisting her massive head around, she caught her husband's eye. "Ready my love?"

He said nothing, merely gripped the long sword tighter.

She knew from Lanni's story, she'd most likely be able to pass through the shield unharmed, but the plan was still risky. They had to try though, otherwise the barrier would never come down.

Determination setting her scales, she flapped her wings hard and headed in. Pulling up, she took in a breath, rolled onto her back and clutched her talons around Tom a bit tighter. If this failed and she burst into flames, he might survive with the protection. Folding her wings across her stomach to add another layer, she dropped from the sky like a stone...

***

They arrived on the roof just as Grams dropped through the covering. The coloring shifted to a blue and she twisted over, her scales shimmering under the returning green hue as her wings billowed out.

She momentarily disappeared behind an office building then came around the other side. Her wings flapped once, twice to gain altitude and she headed their direction.

"What the hell is she doing?" Fallon asked.

Fyris came up next to her. "I have no idea, but she must have a plan."

The oldest of matriarchs hovered into position and dropped Gramps from her talons. The older man landed with a thump, waiting for Grams to shift and join him. She did and strode confidently across the tiny pebbles under their feet.

To the right, the energy beam continued to glow and pulse, waiting for the next victim to feed it.

The pair stopped in front of them, a serene smile on both their faces.

"What are you two doing?" she asked again.

Grams stepped forward, clasping her hands. "We've taught you well Fallon. I hope you'll remember we both loved you deeply and dearly."

Something wasn't right here. She could see it in the glow on Grams face when the beam pulsed again.

"Grams, what..."

But she wasn't listening and cut a look toward Fyris. "You take care of our girl, you hear me?"

Fyris gulped, hard. "Yes M'Lady. She will want for nothing."

The older woman who'd been more of a mother to her than anything else, let go of her hands and tucked one into the crook of her husband's arm. "Shall we dear?"

Tom smiled. "Yes, we shall."

Realization cut through her chest like a knife and she surged forward, but Fyris grabbed her and held her back. "No! No! You can't!"

As a pair they turned toward the beam and without a backward glance, walked into it...

Chapter Twenty-Four

"How could you let them do that!?"

Fyris approved of his *Kyleri's* anger. He felt it just as strongly and gave only answer he could. "It was part of the deal with Golix," he said quietly.

She whipped around, eyes narrowed. "What!?"

"When he brought you here, she negotiated our release with a promise that she would make the shield permanent in your place." The fight went out of her at that and he took her in his arms, stroking her back. "I tried to dissuade them, promised to rescue you myself, but a Dragon's word is sacred and once given is unbreakable."

Her shoulders shook and grief swelled across their connection.

"Take heart human," Arin Manus said softly. "It did not work."

Fallon lifted her head from his chest. "What?"

She was saying that a lot but he lifted her chin with a finger. "The shield is failing," he said, nodding toward the window of the boarding room they'd taken refuge in.

She rotated toward it just as the green hue lightened another shade. "I'll be damned," she whispered. "Why do you think that is?"

He tucked his arms around her again, propping his chin atop her head. "I am no magic user, but I could guess her power is too much for it."

"Either way, it is coming down," Haydn added to his statement. "We have already spotted several places where holes have appeared. It is only a matter of time now."

"So, what are we waiting for? Let's get back there and roust those bastards for good!"

Haydn chuckled and jerked a thumb at Fallon. "I like her."

He did too, loved her in fact but right now they needed to wait for the others. Despite the mayhem they'd created earlier, the Ogre's and Orc's had regrouped and fallen back. It would be best to wait until the Dragons could penetrate the shield and lend a talon in the cleanup.

***

Carax trotted around the throne room.

This wasn't his fault. This was his father's doing, not his and he'd be damned if he got blamed for it.

The communication activated and Golix's long snout parted in a smile. "Tell me of our victory my son."

He snorted. "There is nothing to tell! You have failed. The shield is coming down, not staying up."

"What? How? How did you let this happen?"

He cracked a hoof against the floor. "I let nothing happen! And I am done with your scheming and plotting. I will do this on my own."

Golix actually seemed shocked by his words, which was fine. He was done with all this. It was time for a more direct approach. Slamming a hoof into the computer station, it sparked and sputtered, cutting off whatever else his father might have wanted to say.

Yes, time for action indeed. If he couldn't rule this city, no one would! He turned to the nearest Satyr, barking orders. "Take me to the warehouse."

227

***

"Where do you think you're going..."

Fyris looked up at Fallon's comment, puzzled. "What was that *Kyleri*?"

She frowned over the edge of the monitor then dropped her eyes back to it. "That bastard is going somewhere," she murmured. "I don't want him escaping."

He rose off the couch and moved around to see what she was talking about. On the screen, she was playing back a file and he cocked his head. "Is that Lalum?"

"Yeah," she frowned, rewinding the vid again. "Along with two others. They just left the Tower." She clicked at some of the keys and an overlay of the city came up. Two red dots appeared, moving rapidly down the paved avenues. "Where are you going?"

He shared a look with Arin. "We should follow."

The Chimera's brow pinched. "How? The streets are crawling with the enemy."

He took Fallon's hand, dragging her up out of the chair she'd spent the last rotation in. "We fly."

A few heartbeats later, they drifted along the air currents. He kept one eye on the vehicles below and the other out for signs of pursuit. There was none, thankfully and he spun toward an empty roof only after the two trucks rolled into a building on the city's west side.

Fallon slipped from his talons and Arin and Haydn landed next to them.

It was the Orc that spoke. "I have seen them come here before."

"What do you suppose is inside?"

A new voice rumbled out of the shadows. "Something that never should have been created..."

Haydn and Arin spun, both drawing the swords from their backs.

He whipped around as well, claws out and he could hear Fallon sucking in air, ready to blast whomever it was.

A humanoid eased into the daylight, hands held wide. He was bald, with the red-orange eyes typical of a Dragon. Four long knives hung from a bandolier on his chest, two sword hilts stuck up over his shoulders and two crossbows thumped against his thighs. "Easy, I am not the enemy. Decia sent me."

Fallon stepped around him. "How do we know that?"

A brown eyebrow quirked up. "Because if she did not, you would already be dead." He moved to the edge of the roof. "Now, if you will excuse me, there is business I must attend too."

Fallon swallowed. "Wait," she called out. "What's your name?"

From his perch on the lip, he smiled. "Rixon," he said just before he disappeared over the side.

He rushed forward, leaning out to see where the Dragon had gone, but he was gone.

And a heartbeat later, the warehouse exploded...

***

Azon heard the rumble in the distance seconds

before it rattled the pane of glass.

Mithrin jerked awake, scrubbing a hand down his face. "What was that?"

She shrugged, stroking the back of Rygan's hand and willing him to open his eyes. "I do not know," she answered honestly.

Mithrin headed for the door. "I will see, stay here."

She rattled her chains. "I am not going anywhere."

It was the first time in an age she was free to be even remotely sarcastic and it felt good. Would have been even better if she wasn't still wearing them. Nothing had changed though, and she continued her silent vigil at Rygan's side. She scooted closer, reaching out to the limit of her cuffs to stroke a finger down his face.

Only her hand went further than it had in a hundred Suns and quite literally poked him. She stared at it for a long moment, not believing what she was seeing as the cuff she'd worn almost her entire life, fell away.

The other one followed and the larger, thicker one around her neck parted with a hiss and dropped into her lap...

***

Rygan opened his eyes, expecting to see the stone walls as always. Instead a pair of wood beams greeted him. Confused, he rolled his head to the side to take in the room. Something he hadn't been able to do in some time and was surprised to find a sedate looking bedroom.

A blond haired head lay against the blankets over

him and he recognized Azon, despite the fact her face was buried in the crook of her arm.

Shakily he stroked her hair and she jerked awake. Rubbing the sleep from her eyes, she smiled widely. "Hello."

She wasn't wearing her chains and he feared this was nothing more than a dream. "You, are, free?"

She scooted forward, grabbing his hand between her warm ones. "We both are."

He reached up and touched the ever present medallion around his neck. He wasn't quite, but at least he was no longer being tortured...

***

Phara listened to the news report, smiling across the room at Lanni. "Sounds like they have taken back Bra'ka."

Lanni didn't look up from the piles of paper. "Uh huh."

She gave Tian's arm a squeeze, rose and shifted around the bed to see what had the human woman so distracted. "What have you been doing?"

Lanni paused, tapped the writing stick against her chin and frowned. "And if I add in the coefficient of twelve, multiply that by a, and then divide again by sixteen that should..." She heaved a sigh and scratched out the formula. "No, no, that won't work either."

"Lanni!"

She finally looked up, eyes slightly glazed and Phara tried again. "What are you doing?"

"Oh, erm, well, see here's the thing. Golix has already proven he can travel back and forth between

231

worlds at will, so I'm trying to figure out how he does it," she said in a rush. She dipped back to the papers and started writing again.

Phara reached out and put a hand over hers. "It is magic my friend. Not science."

Lanni shook her head. "No, no, there is science in everything. It is just a matter of finding which kind he's using. If I can do that, maybe I can reverse..."

There were tears in the woman's eyes and she could understand that. She'd felt much the same when she thought Tian was dying and even though he had yet to wake up, he was here and alive.

Lanni felt guilty for Draven's death, it was clear as mud and she got that too. What she'd done in reaction to Arin's supposed death still made her shiver. She'd almost killed an innocent in Haydn the Orc and that still unnerved her. Nothing she could do about it, but still, it was unsettling.

She squeezed Lanni's fingers. "You cannot change the past, no matter how much we may want too."

Lanni jerked away. "Yes, yes I can dammit! And I will!"

She sat on the covers. "The King is dead. It is not your fault."

The woman snorted, silver eyes flaring with anger. "I *know* that. That's not what I'm trying to do. I can't bring anyone back from the dead."

She nodded toward the woman's notes. "Then what are you doing?" she asked for a third time.

Lanni's hands slammed onto the pile, sending a few floating up into the air. "I'm trying to figure out how to open a portal. I want to drop a bomb right on that sumbitches head!"

***

Terra landed on the King's Tower six rotations later to a Heroes fanfare.

Arin, Haydn, her distant cousin Fallon, Fyris and Mithrin stood waiting, along with a youngish looking blonde haired woman she'd never seen before.

She dropped Lanni and Phara from her claws and gently laid Arin between them. A team of Harpies gathered him up and put him on a stretcher so he could be taken to the Shi-so.

Introductions were made and the group headed down to the lower levels, more specifically one of the conference rooms on the 30th floor.

She asked her first question as they settled around the table. "Where's Cannis?"

"Unknown," Arin replied. "He disappeared when the warehouse exploded."

She gazed expectantly around the group. "And the rest of the Unicorns?"

"We know Lalum is dead," Azon, the young blonde explained. "Otherwise I would still be in chains."

Fallon spoke next. "We don't know about the two with him. We only found one body, so it's entirely possible and probably they escaped."

She directed her next question to Azon, having gotten her story and relationship during the elevator ride. "Can all your kind cast portals?"

The humanoid sighed softly. "It varies. Some can. Some cannot. It usually takes more than one, in all truth, but with enough power, a lone member is capable of it."

"What about you?"

The poor thing smiled. "I do not know. It has been a very long time since I had my magic. My fath, Golix," she amended. "Stripped me of it when he trapped me like this."

"Is there a way to reverse it?"

Azon waved it away. "Do not worry about me. I am used to this. Besides, you do have bigger problems."

She was afraid of that and had already speculated such, if only to herself on the flight from Kyles. But, still, she asked mainly because the woman had been on the inside of this mess for a very long time. "Like what?"

Azon's long finger tapped the table top to empathize her point. "Golix's virus was an experiment here, to see if it would work. He plans to do the same in your world." Her chin jerked toward Fallon. "That was what he needed her for. She was supposed to crack into the…" She paused and her cousin supplied the word she needed.

"Central Reserve?"

"Yes, that." She smiled. "Thank you. As I was saying, he needed her to crack their code or something so he could plant the same virus there."

She turned toward Fallon. "Is that possible?"

Her cousin's eyes widened. "Holy shit. That's it. And now it makes sense."

"What does?"

"Lalum's offer. He wanted me to back hack the same network, putting him in charge of the funding Golix would receive for the cure…"

Ok, she was lost, completely. "What?"

Fallon waved a hand, frustration on her features. "Once Golix releases the virus, he'll have the only cure and he plans to sell it to the highest bidder."

She sat, ok, more like collapsed into the chair at the head of the table. All of Golix's planning and scheming, all the years he spent guiding this world along far enough to capture the DNA and ultimately make his way to her world fell into place.

He'd need the funding from Bra'ka, what he'd taken originally to her world, to buy up a company powerful enough to have the access he wanted.

After that, he would have to find a copy of the common cold there, return it here and begin the testing phase. Which they had done, unintentionally, with Draven. He'd dropped the bombs on Rosau to get their attention, knowing they'd take the devices and try to engineer a counter for it.

There was no doubt in her mind he still had someone on the inside of this mess and he undoubtedly now had samples from Draven's reaction. Something Zentai said, about Draven's rare, recessive gene clicked through her thoughts.

That was it! That was what he'd been after this whole time. It had to be...

They'd been played...from the beginning and that sent fury coursing through every nerve she had.

With a deep breath, she stood, eyeing every person at the table. "I'm tired of this. Here's what we're going to do. Fallon, you and Fyris are going back home. Take Lanni and Mithrin with you. You'll need my sister's smarts. Find Golix, who's probably moved by now and stop him. Once you have, bring that son of bitch back here."

Fallon's eyes lit up and the first true smile parted her lips. "With pleasure cousin. I owe that bastard, for

Grams."

She agreed and turned toward Arin. "You and Haydn, head for home. They'll need your help in rebuilding Rosau."

The Chimera she'd not really gotten a chance to know all that well, gave her a respectful nod. "If you are sure, my Queen. I could stay here."

She reached over and patted his shoulder. "No. You served Draven well but you are needed elsewhere."

"What of me?" Azon asked.

She tapped the table. "You are staying right here. I'm going to pick your brain for everything you know."

The woman cracked a tired looking smile. "As long as you do not put me in chains, I am happy to oblige."

"And me?" Phara asked.

"When Tian is better, I want you two scouring the land. Those bastards are still out there and until they're all dead, none of us are safe."

The Naiad grinned widely. "It will be my utmost pleasure to hunt them down."

"What about you sis?" Lanni asked quietly.

She gazed out the window at the nearly ruined city beyond. Draven had tasked her with ruling in his place and she wasn't going to let him down. "I will be here. Where I am needed..."

***

Doctor Zentai jammed the needle into the subject's upper arm, drawing yet another sample at the Master's request. He shivered in the cold room and went about his duty quickly. Why Golix needed more blood or bone marrow was beyond him, but he wasn't paid to ask questions, merely do what he was told. He finished up as quickly as he shaking feathers allowed and stashed the specimens in his lab coat.

Pausing at the door, he gazed back at the poor Dragon, not wishing this fate on anyone as the singular machine in the room pumped air into his lungs with a long, drawn out hiss...

The End

For now...

Margaret Taylor

About Margaret Taylor

Margaret Taylor currently lives in San Antonio, TX and is scratching post for her five cats. She is an avid writer, a novice photographer and enjoys all things Paranormal, Fantasy and Science Fiction! Just ask her, she'll tell you!

⁂

<u>A First Love Never Dies</u> - Book 1 of The Spi-Corp Series (Sci-Fi Romance)

<u>Saving His Love</u> – Book 2 of The Spi-Corp Series (Sci-Fi Romance)

To Light The Dragon's Fire – Book 1 of the Dragons, Griffons and Centaurs, Oh My! Series (Fantasy Romance)

To Save The Broken Heart – Book 2 of the Dragons, Griffons and Centaurs, Oh My! Series (Fantasy Romance)

<u>Wolf's Paradox</u> - Book 1 of The Layren Series (Paranormal Romance)

<u>I Saw Momma Shoot Santa Claus</u> – Book 1 of The Legacy Series (Paranormal Romance)

<u>All In The Name Of Love</u> (Contemporary Romantic Suspense)

<u>Love's Prophecy</u> (Paranormal Romance)

To Free The Dragon's Soul

The Seer – Book 1 of The Shadowcon Series (Urban Fantasy)

With a little something for everyone, if you visit her blog and ask nicely, she might be persuaded to post some tasty excerpts from many of her other projects! *Bring Cookies as payment please!*

If you've enjoyed this or any of Margaret other works, please, 𐑀𐑀𐑀𐑀 𐑀 𐑀𐑀𐑀𐑀𐑀 . The greatest compliment Authors can receive is hearing from the fans.

And feel free to connect with her on:

Facebook
Twitter
Blog
Email